Precious BLOODLINE

Kiss of a New World Order

ARTICA BURR

ISBN 979-8-89121-759-1 (softcover)
ISBN 979-8-89121-760-7 (hardcover)
ISBN 979-8-89121-761-4 (ebook)
Library of Congress Control Number: 2023913659

Printed in the United States of America.

Artica Burr Publications
5040 Kraus Road
Clarence, NY 14031

OTHER BOOKS BY ARTICA BURR

Billy Bender and the Red Hot Ants
(Artica Burr Publications, USA)

Hockey Legend Myth and Verse
(Trafford Publishing, Canada)

INTRODUCTION

Through the Author's Windshield

My ancestors emerged from some rather intriguing areas in Europe. My grandparent's generation was the first in our family to brave the ocean blue and arrive at America's shores. Those related to them trickled in or stayed behind. By the end of WW2, few family relations were left in Europe. It appears to be due to the war and a lack of related boys born to carry the surname. Interestingly, during wartime in Europe, many people moving from various countries lacked proper paperwork, and although couples produced children, they could not formally wed without those papers. Thus many surnames fell to be maternal and near impossible to trace as ancestry.

After dabbling around with family history and personal family tales, I began investigating the locations mentioned, which became likened to a short ride on a wild horse on a dead-end road ending cliffside. The areas were laced with a tremendous amount of religious turbulence. Further, I always pay attention to articles concerning the emergence of the negative bloodline but find no solid explanation other than it happened around 25,000 years ago.

During spring planting in my garden, idle thoughts caused everything to churn together, yielding a story thick with fiction that I could spread onto paper like jam on toast. I kept planting seeds and ideas; the story bloomed and grew like a vine with twists and turns. My family research yielded a perfect setting in France, although truthfully, the location is innocent of being tied to my story by any thread of truth. I sprinkled in some local US places I have personally visited.

An eerie moment occurred when I began browsing through photos for a possible book cover. I was stunned to find that captured in a photograph, there they were. The portrayal was identical to what I had seen in my mind's eye. Needless to say, it was a time-stopping moment. To my great surprise, it appears the professional photo might have been taken in Ukraine, which at this point in time is currently mired in conflict.

I could tell that my choice for the book cover would be perfect. I toyed with the idea of taking a similar staged photo and had a charming girl in mind. I then realized that no one would want to be photographed as her husband once I alluded to the storyline. Read the novel, and you will understand my remark perfectly.

In a fashion, the moral of this story is: that you can't tell a book by its cover. The couple on the book cover both express the possibility of an ongoing relationship. If I may better clarify the moral: Consent to it, Live through it. It is perhaps not wise to dive into marriage after a short courtship.

Read on and enjoy the ride.

CONTENTS

CHAPTER ONE

A dark, foreboding cloud of frustration continued to loom over Clarisse as it had over the past month. During her private moments, it grew thicker and drew tighter around her, always edging into her thoughts. It bestowed upon Clarisse its unwanted gifts of doubt, rejection, and loss of confidence. This morning in the mirror, her quandary was clearly etched upon her twenty-six-year-old face. Her usually bright blue eyes were devoid of spark and had diminished to a dull shade of gray. Not a shred of marital bliss reflected back at her, nor had there been any.

Clarisse had taken a rapid backslide into looking as she did when her parents had suddenly passed away. Clarisse's initial enthusiasm over being a newlywed had seriously waned. It seemed evident that the harder she tried to please Roger, her new husband, the further he stepped back and placed a barrier between them. The marital bliss she had visualized, which would have supplied her need for comfort, had evaporated into thin air.

She addressed her mirror reflection, "For better or worse, but you look like the depths of worse are swallowing you whole for breakfast. Exactly how much deeper are you going to let the worse part get? You better find the exact problem and fix this before it meets the point of no return. You must have failed. It's up to you to change things back to what they were."

Clarisse fully understood that marriage was a give-and-take proposition. A comfortable relationship between her parents had sheltered her youth. She was not hesitant to give, but Roger was firmly unwilling to receive. The next few days would be challenging to face. The separation Roger embedded between them became glaring when he worked locally instead of out of town.

Clarisse had come to welcome a block of time away from Roger to mull over the situation. But to date, she only accomplished being driven to tears and a dark-seated feeling of being overwhelmed. During the weeks since her wedding, an ominous abstract feeling had crept into her troubled realm and begun to lurk within her. A growing instinctual sensation that something painful was hidden and the problem could be beyond her repair. It had begun to deny her any attempt at serenity. Clarisse knew she needed to seek out what went awry. She was determined to resolve whatever the root of the problem was and get things back to where they were before the wedding. If the blame were hers, she would accept the responsibility. The Roger she dealt with now seemed to be a vacated shell of the warm and affectionate man she had fallen in love with. Clarisse longed to have the Roger she had known return.

Clarisse acknowledged that if her parents were alive, her choice of rushed civil marriage rather than a church wedding would have never happened. After the fact, she recognized that she had also disappointed herself in her moments of weakness. But the unsettling sensation hovering around her seemed to run deeper than only the guilt over not following the dictates of her faith and what her parents would have approved of. She needed to grasp whatever disrupted their relationship, examine it, and find a solution; however, to date, it remained elusive. She quickly brushed several tears away, inhaled to steady herself, and began to get dressed and ready for her scheduled appointment.

It became clear to Clarisse that it was necessary, no matter how distressing, that she step back and objectively examine the chain of events that had occurred. She would need to find the problem to attempt to fix the situation. She must have slipped and done something that changed the course of their relationship. She was determined to correct whatever wrong she committed and bring Roger back to the charming man she fell in love with. While other newly married couples were no doubt constantly worried about unexpected conception, Clarisse remained in limbo, with the study door functioning as an established barrier between her lying alone in their bed and Roger on the couch in his study. Roger's version of living as one was a surprise twist of words. Roger had made that choice without explaining or discussing it with her. The warmth of Roger's arms had drifted away and was on its way to becoming a memory. Either she had somehow failed bitterly, or perhaps the distance that had grown between them was based on a misunderstanding.

It was early in the day, yet barely six AM. Clarisse reached for a cereal box just as the coffee maker growled its conclusion. Concentrated thoughts concerning her problems usually brought on a nagging headache. To cover that possibility, she tossed a medication in her purse. "Damn this economy," she thought out loud. It was hard to feel any confidence and move forward when every segment of her life was taking a turn for the worse. She decided to pick up today's employment newspaper and look for a job opening while waiting for her appointment.

The accounting firm had lost the majority of its smaller clients. Clarisse could understand their need to lay her off. The last hires are always likely to take the clip if revenues get tight. But she lacked confidence in the local New York economy rapidly turning an about-face and her old job being reinstated. After having two years of dependable work given to the firm, it seemed as though they could have given her more warning than a Friday short notice layoff and handing her the vacation pay owed her. She had insisted on a written letter of recommendation and waited there after the day's end until she received it. Clarisse was inches away from taking her CPA exam. She felt relieved that the firm had already covered all of her educational expenses and prepaid her exam fees. Clarisse had been both grateful and surprised that, at the point of her termination, they had not required her reimbursement of the tuition and fees they had prepaid on her behalf. As she looked back upon it, Clarisse realized that the termination was almost apologetic on the part of the firm.

Roger's response to her bringing home the news of her being unemployed had taken her aback. Clarisse had elected to bring the matter to light during dinner, which was the only time they spent one-on-one.

Clarisse recalled her words, "This afternoon, I became the latest victim of the hollowing out of the New York State economy. I'm close to taking my CPA exam and can accelerate that date. It should create more opportunities for me as I seek new employment," Clarisse had quickly added. "I can wrap up my studies and be a CPA well before we have to file our joint taxes." Clarisse had been hoping to gain more financial information about her husband when tax time rolled around. She had never seen a pay stub or a bank statement since everything was locked away in his briefcase or the study. There had been silence while she waited to see Roger's reaction to the news.

"I was single most of the year. I intend to file separately. Your employer would have retained you if the company had been impressed with your work skill set." Roger had replied, not even glancing her way. After a brief pause, he had continued, "Don't plan on any household financial help on my part. I have my own obligations. Due to your newly acquired financial woes, in addition to finding new employment, it's an opportune time for you to sell your parent's house. Until then I highly suggest that the rent of that house be increased. The rental amount you are charging that family of your church friends only covers our monthly apartment rent. You had better recognize your need to raise the rent until the house is sold. Real estate taxes will be due shortly," Roger had stated.

"I will add the sale proceeds to my account for a future house purchase."

Clarisse's face flushed concerning his remark about her competency. Although it was a first-time experience, Clarisse had decided to hold her ground politely and cautiously. "Actually, Clare and Tom are saving and hoping to buy the place, but they need another year of saving for a down payment," Clarisse had countered. "I have not made up my mind to sell the house, but if I did, I was considering holding a mortgage for them."

A perturbed look had flashed across Roger's face. "Personally holding the mortgage is out of the question. A clean sale and cash in the bank is the best solution, especially since you are far too attached to the past. I will call a realtor tomorrow."

Clarisse had quickly responded, "Please don't rush to do that. I need to think things over. I need time to decide what I would like to do."

Roger had immediately got up and dropped his cloth napkin on the supper table with finality. "Since when have wives not listened to their husbands' advice?" He then went to his study and locked the door behind him.

Clarisse mulled over Roger's response as she added more creamer and then sipped her coffee. It seemed to her that Roger was apparently hung up on the words love, honor, and obey instead of love, honor, and cherish. She had only rented the house to give herself time to adjust to the loss of her parents. It was a lovely, charming house with no mortgage. Clarisse felt that, at some point, she might want to return to living there or keep it as a rental home. The family renting it treated the property with great respect. They would be her first choice as a buyer if she chose to sell the house. It was her family home. If she parted with her parent's home, Clarisse felt she might decide to use some of the money to open a CPA practice.

Clarisse sighed and suddenly felt foolish paying for the apartment expenses with no contribution from Roger, but she had agreed to that arrangement when Roger also had an apartment. She hesitated to go back on her word. It was her name on the apartment lease. It seemed proper that she remain responsible, but a terse thought came to mind. If they bought a home at an as yet undetermined price, was Roger expecting her to continue the current bill pay arrangement and make the mortgage payments on the new house? Roger had expensive tastes. She shuddered and quickly swept that thought off the table, along with a couple of cereal crumbs. The problem in their relationship most certainly happened before the eventful loss of her employment.

It was still an early hour. Clarisse turned her mind in the direction of her current endeavor. At the moment, fifteen hundred dollars was a small fortune. Before she met Roger, she'd completed medical trials during college. The usual fees paid were fifty or seventy-five dollars. Whatever this study was, it could prove to be a treasure of opportunity arriving right at her doorstep during her time of need. It was precisely the dollar amount she needed to help her easily coast past the rest of the month while she looked for new employment. If she could trim down the budget and include her vacation pay, there was an excellent chance she would have enough money left over for the taxes on her parent's home. Desperately, Clarisse vowed that during her period of unemployment, she would settle her mind and apply her attention to her studies for her CPA exam. If she failed to pass the exam the first time, additional fees would be charged for a retake.

Clarisse shuffled her thoughts and returned to the difficulties at hand. She admitted that she should have told Roger her intentions and where she was going this morning. At least a note on the kitchen blackboard could be left, but it probably wouldn't matter because she'd be back long before he returned from work. Yet another disappointment would be laid upon her if she was rejected for participation in the clinical trial. At this point, any new failure on her part was undoubtedly best left unmentioned to her husband. Clarisse sighed heavily. It didn't matter if she didn't deliberately do anything wrong. Her doing anything right seemed to have slipped beyond her grasp and ability.

Clarisse continued her breakfast, choosing a container of yogurt from the refrigerator. She had no idea how long she would be at her appointment. Cereal was likely less than a hardy breakfast choice. The thought occurred to her that if she arrived earlier than her appointed time, she could shorten her appointment wait time. After checking the projected weather and finding a brutal temperature forecast, she changed her clothes to more relaxed attire. She unplugged the coffee pot, defiantly glanced at the blackboard, resolved not to leave a note, and left the air-conditioned apartment to face the heat of the day.

CHAPTER TWO

The frame of her old, faithful, navy Toyota groaned in protest when Clarisse swung open the driver's side door. A blast of searing dry heat hit her squarely in the face. Tributaries of perspiration began rolling down the back of her neck, seeking their way toward the river already beginning to flow down her spine. The heat was constant and unbearable even with the door open. She glanced at the letter she had received in the mail, quickly keyed the address into her GPS, and checked the results. She couldn't justify wasting the fuel. Her destination was only six blocks north of their apartment. Despite the heat, it was undoubtedly a manageable walk, and she had plenty of time.

Clarisse got back out of the car, sighed, slammed the door shut, locked her car, and tossed the keys into her purse. She studied herself in the car window as she pulled her blonde-streaked hair off of her damp neck. Clarisse decided to wrap it into a loose ponytail, hoping to gain a bit of refuge from the heat. She would have welcomed even the slightest breeze, but the continual lack of motion in the air had left temperatures stagnant for weeks.

Her gaze was drawn to the crystal rosary beads that hung from her rearview mirror. They sparkled as they captured the morning sunlight. The rosary swung methodically back and forth as if to count the passage of time. It became a reminder that she had skipped church services once again this week. Clarisse reaffirmed that had her parents been alive to witness the new life she had plunged into, her hasty marriage and her violation of church law would never have occurred.

As she stepped onto the sidewalk, Clarisse's thoughts continued drifting. The Friday she became unemployed, Clarisse had succumbed to the need to stop at the Basilica for a moment of prayer, even at the risk of running into Father David. Her footsteps had echoed as she walked down a side aisle, intent on lighting a candle. She had come to the church craving guidance concerning the new state of current events affecting her life. The church had been empty but for a few other visitors dotting the pews, lost in their silent discourse. The familiar and comfortable scents of the burning beeswax candles and a faint trace of burned incense had engulfed her. But she had found no flood of the internal comfort she was seeking and customarily found. During those moments, she had become sharply aware of the barrier that her growing guilt placed between her and the ability to fully practice her faith.

Clarisse continued her walk and began to review her relationship with Father David. Her closeness to the church seemed to have become an issue of dislike on Roger's part.

Clarisse felt sure Father David was aware that she had disregarded his advice and opted to marry Roger in a civil ceremony. The priest had broken contact with her after the newspaper had publicly posted a photo spread of her marriage to Roger. The chain of events posed confusion for Clarisse. She was unsure if Roger had deliberately swayed her away from following the dictates of her religion or if it was she that should take the entire blame for contradicting the faith her parents had nurtured in her since her birth. The unexpected publicity of her wedding might have been deemed a slap in the pastor's face, but she had not expected the news coverage and had no control over the extensive press coverage.

The sudden tragic loss of both of her parents had left Clarisse on the brink of a bottomless abyss. With no family to turn to, Father David had helped her through the funeral arrangements. He had encouraged her to rely on the church and her faith for her desperately needed comfort. It was only after numerous visits to the rectory and the church that she had begun to stabilize her grief enough to a point where she could feign normal function.

She had come to trust Father David's advice and deeply appreciated his kindness. But in the matter of her marriage, Clarisse had chosen to disregard the priest's cautionary tone. Father David had remained firm in his belief that she should not rush into marriage with someone she had only known for several months. The priest had expressed concerns that important issues might be clouded for Clarisse since she was still in a state of grief over the relatively recent loss of her parents. But Roger had won Clarisse over by promising her that at a later date, they could be remarried in a church wedding. Her compelling need to seek comfort in his arms and begin a new life had resulted in her agreement that, for now, they should start their lives together by settling for an immediate civil ceremony.

Clarisse had promised herself that she would correct her recently lapsed church attendance, even if Roger continued to claim the excuse that he was too busy to attend church services with her. During the past weeks, she had considered attending services in a different parish. But lately, Clarisse reasoned that the only right thing to do was confess to Father David about her choice rather than avoid the issue and her family priest. The haunting truth was that she would also have to admit that the priest appeared absolutely correct in his advice. Clarisse was ready to accept that she did not know enough about Roger and should have delayed their wedding. But she also needed to clarify the current situation in their marriage because she fully expected Father David to inquire about what was transpiring. After a month of marriage, she still knew no further details about her husband's past life or current personal endeavors. It was hard to admit that she only knew the minor remnants of his past that Roger had mentioned during their brief courtship. She could never bring herself to discuss with Father David that Roger was avoiding the consummation of their marriage despite weeks now passing since the wedding. But surely the priest would notice her unhappy state by her stressful look.

Since their civil ceremony, in numerous ways, Roger had expressed that she was too attached to her faith. He indicated his approval of her stepping back from weekly church attendance.

Roger had directly spoken the sentiment on a Sunday over supper. "Clarisse, it's good to see that you are not leaning as heavily on your faith and attachment to the church. It is better to learn to deal with life's stark realities. Staying steeped in your family's traditions won't help you achieve the balance you lack."

Clarisse's stomach had tightened. She needed a prospective date for their church wedding in order to approach Father David and demonstrate her desire to heal her breach with the church. "Knowing the dates you are available for a church wedding is needed so I can plan with Father David," Clarisse softly sighed and responded. "You did commit to Father David and also to me that we would arrange to arrive at a date you would be available."

Roger abruptly got up from the supper table. "I have no idea what my schedule is months in advance, which is how your church and your Father David insist on operating to schedule weddings. I fail to see my employers bending to accommodate a second wedding since they attended our original wedding and paid for it." That said, Roger went to his study and firmly locked the door behind him.

During the last weeks, Clarisse had felt herself grasping after the shreds of confidence she had struggled to gain since the loss of her parents. Clarisse had thought the marriage would be a positive change and lift her into a new and meaningful life. Clarisse felt that her life, which she had structured upon the pillars of faith, trust, and love, had become an existence filled with uncertainty. She was now faced with isolation from the church, a distant husband, no one to turn to, and the unexpected loss of employment. If Roger intended to pull her away from the church, he certainly was not presenting a tempting alternative.

Clarisse brushed those thoughts aside and continued walking. She could have used a stiff dose of air conditioning to help revive her, but in the matter of traveling only six blocks, the old Toyota would have still only considered a suggestion of cooler air. She reasoned that most public buildings had cooling units turned on, at least in some fashion. Sitting and waiting in even a poor excuse for air-conditioning might feel at least a bit more comfortable. Since Clarisse had plenty of time until her appointment, she resigned herself that the clinic was within walking distance and that she had made the right decision to walk there. With the current unknowns facing her, every penny counted.

Today's weather forecast was in the high nineties. It had been hot last night again, and already this morning, she could feel waves of heat rising from the sidewalk. The soles of her sandals began to feel paper thin and useless against the hot concrete. For nearly two months, the heat had been continuously unbearable. There was talk about mandatory electric brownouts if voluntary reduction of electric consumption did not improve. The entire Northeastern US was suffering day and night under the unmerciful, searing weather. She moved off the sidewalk when she could and walked on the burnt-out grass, which crackled beneath her every step.

As far as her eye could see, the extended dry season had caused the ground surface to vein, intertwining into an endless mosaic pattern. The weeds in the lawns, which usually flaunted themselves still green in hot temperatures, had lost the battle and shriveled up into dry, nearly invisible nubs. Even the sturdy dandelions had utterly lost the will to try. The yards along the street looked as parched of purpose as Clarisse's daily life. Volunteering at the conservatory had become likened to leaving the Sahara desert and entering an oasis.

There had been those at work who had hotly debated the weather situation during lunch breaks. Some felt the weather was being deliberately manipulated. They made the valid point that government patents were held for precisely that purpose. A lot of their thinking made sense when Clarisse considered the profit to be made. Food prices had continued to escalate. A lot of money could be made by controlling the commodities market. It appeared they were seeding the sky overhead, but none of the needed rainfall materialized. When there was a promise of rain, more planes arrived overhead; the clouds dissipated or moved on. Many of her former coworkers had concluded that a war for the dollar was being waged against the general public. They were adamant that weather control was part of that war.

Clarisse had never offered comments during the lunchroom discussions. But she had started to mull their arguments further after reading an article stating that the Great Lakes water level had dropped several feet. The lack of rain had only made water resources more valuable. There appeared to be a thrust to privatize water ownership. Worldwide vast land purchases above the locations of aquifers had been made. Clarisse had found the thought of everyone being made a financial victim over a basic need, not to mention the upset to the balance of nature. The issue was unsettling, to say the least.

The concept that unstoppable deception could be forcing its way into her daily life gave Clarisse an involuntary shudder. Her life had always revolved around honesty, trust, and fundamental truths. Although being unemployed would lend her the time to research the weather matter, she felt hesitant to examine things further out of fear of what the facts might reveal. Rather than do anything that might heap more stress upon her, Clarisse forced herself to concentrate on resolving her immediate personal problems. The rest of the pending trouble in the world would have to wait until her daily life had stabilized.

As she attempted to avoid the intense heat of the sidewalk, she conceded to the underlying reason that she had not left Roger a note. She had every right to make a personal decision whether to participate in the trial or decline it. It would be better for her alone to make the judgment rather than be powerless to refuse because Roger might consider the dollars to be gained more important than her right to decide for herself. Trying to maintain her identity within the marriage had become increasingly difficult.

The thought crossed Clarisse's mind that her friend Mary was in a far poorer position than the one she had on hand. Mary had a new baby coming. Her boyfriend was long gone, and then, to top it all off, Mary had gotten a lay-off slip a week before Clarisse did. Mary had only one choice. She had to move back to Iowa and live with her parents. Mary and Clarisse had developed a friendship during their days of employment together. But Mary had become so caught up with the depth of her problems that she had failed to grasp any understanding concerning the personal difficulties that Clarisse had ventured forth and tried to express. Despite the friendship turning more one-sided than it had seemed to be, Clarisse had given Mary several hundred dollars before Mary left to return to Iowa. She hoped Mary would contact her once she settled in with her parents. Mary had been afraid to mention the significant issue of her six-month pregnancy before returning home, feeling she could best explain the matter to her parents in person.

The following week Clarisse's services were also no longer needed at the firm. At least she and Roger still had one income, but Roger was not sharing his revenue. A disturbing, undefined wedge was churning between Clarisse and her new husband. The last few days, Roger had been working locally rather than out of town. The unsettling disconnection between them had continually hung suspended in the air around them. It was far easier to excuse matters and try again when he returned from traveling than to exist, concealing the discontent that painfully festered inside her. Clarisse felt the separation between them echo each time she heard the shart snap when Roger locked his study door or briefcase. The thought crossed her mind that Roger was concealing more than his paperwork and finances. Immediately Clarisse tried to brush the idea away, but it lingered in the back of her mind. Roger did spend a considerable amount of time traveling.

Clarisse took a deep breath and pushed her difficult unanswered questions forward, "Does he regret the marriage?

Has he fallen in love with someone else?" Clarisse had to think things through further. She could not bear to ask those awkward questions to Roger directly. "It has to be something else," she determined.

CHAPTER THREE

Clarisse considered what had transpired over the last months as she continued to walk to her clinical screening appointment. In all honesty, to begin with, she had been made aware that Roger hadn't favored the complications of a church wedding. Clarisse had insisted on it and started planning to use all her meager savings to achieve it. In an effort to set a wedding date in motion, she had invited Father David to sit down with her and Roger at her apartment. The intent was to discuss the required pre-nuptial details concerning the church's paperwork and counseling sessions with the priest. Roger had told her he was of the same faith as she; therefore, Clarisse had assumed that Roger would expect a meeting with the priest would be required.

As it happened, the meeting requested with Father David was held with short notice to Roger and Clarisse. On the date of the meeting, Clarisse had worked through her lunch hour to leave work early. Although Roger had not yet arrived at Clarisse's apartment, the priest had settled comfortably onto a chair at Clarisse's kitchen table. With a cup of freshly brewed coffee in hand, the priest then proceeded to discuss some of the matters simply with Clarisse.

"You make a fine cup of coffee, Clarisse. My housekeeper fails me in that respect," Father David had said. "At Our Lady of Victory, reservations for a wedding date usually are set a year in advance due to the waiting list. Since you and your family have long been parishioners, I can offer you the last remaining Saturday date." The priest had then thumbed through his yearly planner and indicated the available Saturday. "I also brought you a list of the various fees the church charges for weddings at the Basilica. A few of them are optional due to your personal choices."

Clarisse had been ill-prepared to hear that reservations for a church wedding at the Basilica usually had to be made a year in advance. She had only expected a delay of several months. The usual prenuptial counseling did not delay a wedding for such a lengthy time period. Clarisse had looked at the open planner page Father David had indicated. The only Saturday available was eleven months away. In addition, to the date delay, the fees were much higher than she had envisioned. The priest could see Clarisse was showing the normal stunned reaction to the size of the fees.

Father David then explained, "As the Bishop sees things, the Basilica is not just a church, and the fees should reflect the shouldering of the heavy cost of upkeep of a cathedral building. Clarisse, it seems a long time away, but perhaps the date is quite good, considering the loss of your parents is still relatively fresh. Death and marriage are life-changing events that do not affect one lightly. It takes time to grieve. It could be unwise to marry after a relatively short courtship period. By the time the wedding date arrives, you will both have a better understanding of your relationship. What is nearly a year of waiting if you will have a lifetime together?"

It was at that point in their conversation that Roger arrived. Roger was over half an hour late for their meeting. At the sight of the priest sitting at the kitchen table, Roger failed to greet Clarisse. Roger had immediately exhibited an underlying resentment concerning the imposition upon his valuable time. Clarisse had been surprised and embarrassed by Roger's attitude since he knew how helpful Father David had been and continued to be concerning her grief.

In return, upon finally meeting Roger, Father David had not responded warmly to Roger. The priest abruptly appeared uneasy and immediately assumed a formal attitude. "I have explained to Clarisse that the only available Saturday wedding date at the Basilica is months away, a bit over ten months away. I suggested that due to her fairly recent loss, it may be advantageous for both of you to extend your courtship period. In the best of situations, two months is hardly an adequate period of time to prepare for a life-long union and the sacred vows of matrimony."

While Roger appeared briskly polite to the priest, he had brushed the priest's comment aside and excused himself, "I must leave immediately due to a pressing appointment that my work suddenly required of me."

Father David had quickly risen from his chair. "Perhaps your schedule can become more accommodating to the church over the next months," the priest had countered.

Roger had quickly stepped around the priest, advanced to the door, and made his exit. Feeling sick at heart, Clarisse had been left to deal with the throes of her embarrassment.

Father had turned to Clarisse after Roger left. Clarisse recalled his words. "I must remind you, Clarisse, that marriage is a serious commitment. A Catholic marriage is meant to create a strong bond that unites both parties as one in the eyes of the Lord and to create the proper atmosphere to cultivate the faith of any children resulting from that union. Many times one must rely upon the grace of God to see a marriage through life's perilous journey. Indeed, one person's faith is perhaps stronger than the other partner's. Many times this is the case. But a commitment to similar values between both parties is the glue that holds marriages together through life's difficulties and disappointments." Father David had taken her hand. "My child, first impressions many times fall short. I have known you and your family for many years now. I do not sense a parallel depth of your religious commitment in your young man. I see you at services but never the both of you. Search hard for an answer in that respect, and then advise me if you still want to pursue this marriage. Try not to let your grief cloud your good judgment. I cannot promise that your grief will be over within another year. Grief, my child takes its own time. It is always better to wait for sadness to settle before making lifelong decisions."

Clarisse had seen Father David to the door. She had offered the only explanation that she could think of, which had been that Roger was under tremendous pressure at work. Clarisse had promised the priest that she would consider his words.

She then agreed to sit down with Father David sometime the following week and discuss matters further. As it turned out, that meeting never took place. What transpired at the apartment was the only discussion about the marriage that she had with Father David.

Clarisse had always relied heavily upon her faith. The church had helped ease her pain during her acute period of trauma and grief. But meeting Roger had provided a reason for her to reach forward and attempt to adjust to a new segment of her life. Clarisse had no intention of allowing their relationship to replace her faith but rather to join the two aspects of her life as complements, one to the other. She had assumed it would not be difficult to do so since both she and Roger had been raised as Catholics.

Clarisse kept walking and noted that, for some strange reason, their marriage was the issue that caused their entire relationship to disintegrate. It caused a chain reaction of some sort creating a downward spiral.

CHAPTER FOUR

Clarisse continued her walk. She took a deep breath and unleashed the memories of what had transpired that day after the priest left. Mixed emotions aside, she had to examine the exchange between Roger and herself.

Roger had returned to her apartment an hour later with a beautiful rose-colored potted orchid in hand. His tender charms had experienced a full-blown recovery. "Please forgive me for leaving so abruptly," He had said as he offered her the orchid, giving her a loving smile. "At the end of the day, I was told to meet a courier at the airport. He was delivering a sizeable corporate donation for me to hand carry to the Botanical Society at the Buffalo Conservatory. It had to be given to them before they closed for the day. Seeing the waterfall at the Botanical Gardens where we first met gave me a fantastic idea that I could resolve both a problem I had just encountered at work and our wedding plans." Roger had led her over to the couch to sit down beside him.

"At the end of next month, the lease arrangement is up on my corporate apartment. A specific sizeable expense deduction is deducted monthly from my compensation. If I continue my lease, the amount could reduce my pay for the next two years, even if I married you during the new lease period and then vacated my apartment. Since the corporation I work for is a significant contributor to the Botanical Gardens, the administration welcomed the idea of having our wedding there. There would be no cost to use the gardens for the ceremony. They would help us rearrange the area needed with flowers from their gardens. The only expense would be for a caterer if we wanted to have a reception in the conservatory conference room."

Roger then took the orchid from her and set it on the coffee table. Roger had gently drawn her into his arms. He had softly sung several lines of a French song as he stroked the side of her cheek. "What do you think, my love?" Roger had asked, tenderly gazing into her eyes. "You already have your beautiful wedding dress. What better place than one that you love so dearly? You will be a princess surrounded by a special place you and your mother helped make what it is today."

Roger had gone on to explain, "Forgive me if I disappointed your Father David. Unfortunately, the demands made on me are such that my work has become my god. I have been promised I will be moved into the high-ranking level of the company soon. Once that happens, I promise to have the leisure time to attend church with you. Right now, the pressure I am under does not allow for such. Will you forgive me?" As he pressed her close and kissed the side of her neck, he whispered, "My Clarisse, my princess, please, please say you forgive me."

Clarisse had felt the flood of his desire engulf and surround her. Her relief that his attitude had changed caused her to fall into the warmth of the moment and the strength of his arms. It had been difficult for both of them to wait for the bliss of their wedding night. His gushing tenderness had created an overpowering struggle within her. Waiting through long months to consummate their relationship had felt like an overwhelming task. Roger's wedding proposal had heavily tugged at Clarisse's heartstrings.

While Roger awaited her answer, the moments of their first meeting and courtship had rippled through Clarisse's mind. She had donated her time at the Botanical Gardens, as had her mother. The conservatory was located so close to the Basilica that it was a prominent part of the local community. She had gone to the conservatory twice a month since childhood. Clarisse had helped plant much of what grew and thrived there. The turning of each spade of soil had fostered a deep respect for God's green earth within her. The spicy scent of the warm moss and the delightful fine moisture in the air had become part of her life cycle. As she grew taller, so did the ferns, palms, and orchids that she had planted with her mother.

The Botanical Gardens became further endeared as a singularly important part of her life. While placing the newly potted orchids on display for the local Botanical Society Flower Show, Clarisse and Roger first met. She had noticed him as a handsome visitor to the Conservatory several times. On that monumental day, when she had looked up from her work, he had been standing there offering her his charming smile, with interest burning in his dark eyes. He was impeccably dressed. She felt immediately attracted to him.

"Introductions are in order. I am Roger Baudelaire. I have seen that you work very diligently every time I come here," Roger said. "This time, I had the sense to bring you an iced tea in hopes you would take a break so we might share a bit of conversation."

Clarisse had felt flattered that she, in her ordinary dirt-dusted work clothes, had attracted the attention of such an elegant gentleman. "Clarisse Michel-Laurent," she answered wide-eyed and with her innocent smile. She had brushed all the peat moss off her clothes and agreed to leave her workstation.

"There is a touch of dirt on the tip of your nose," Roger cautioned while offering her his handkerchief. "While it is rather charming, it might prove distracting during a serious conversation."

"I best not work so diligently. That happens a lot. Give me a nod when the debris has departed," Clarisse laughed and replied as she patted her nose.

They sat together on one of the welcoming benches for public visitors. That conversation led to her describing their family's trip to Hawaii when she was eight. Clarisse was so enthralled with the wild-growing orchids that it eventually followed that she and her mother achieved years of deep-rooted joy volunteering together at the Conservatory.

At Roger's suggestion, their first date had been a day trip to the Sonnenberg Gardens and the balance of the lovely day spent in Canandaigua, New York. The lush shade gardens immediately adjacent to the conservatory building at Sonnenberg had most certainly managed to survive the heat wave due to constant care.

Clarisse interrupted one of the gardeners, "I volunteer at the conservatory in Buffalo," she said. "How have you kept your plantings in such stunning condition throughout the drought? I wish we could have thriving plantings outside at our entry area."

"I have been to the conservatory you mentioned," the employee replied. "We knew the drought was pending. We dug up all the perennials and spread water retention crystals in the root areas before replanting everything. They expand to four hundred times their size after watering, keeping the roots hydrated. It saves wasting a lot of water. This year there was no extra spillover watering which only grows weeds that require work to remove. Have the conservatory call us if they are interested in information about the product we use and where we purchase it."

The conservatory had thanked Clarisse profusely for the lead on the helpful hydration technique and added the products recommended. The results were impressive.

Clarisse had been immediately enchanted when she entered the building. "The intricacy of the planted stone wall is so charming it appears as though I'm walking into another era in time. The water finding its way over the stones creates such a fresh aroma." Clarisse had laid her hands on the wall as if to prove to herself it was real. "I've learned about touches of creativity in addition to work-saving methods. This is all delightfully inspiring."

"I knew you would appreciate this place because you have the tender heart of a gardener," Roger had said. "It is not as extensive as your Buffalo Conservatory, but it certainly does not lack charm. This wall reminds me of my early youth in French Canada. Beautiful stone buildings with a profusion of gardens were everywhere, which was positively breathtaking. Those places are a fond memory of mine. I seldom daydream, but when I find a moment to spare, I dream of buying an old estate house. I would restore the grand house and grounds to their former glory." Roger had laughed. "Of course, it better have a caretaker house on the property for maintenance since I would have to be tremendously busy earning money to pay for all the restoration and upkeep. I may well have to settle for just something quaint in Saint Catherine's, Canada, with a large courtyard garden, but definitely a stone house."

"It's a lovely dream," Clarisse had replied. "Perhaps size matters in the respect that you need something that will allow you time to enjoy and not worry about constant revenue flow. Of course, it's your decision. That was just the accountant in me sort of leaking forward," Clarisse had said with a smile.

"I realize I might have to scissor down the size of my dream to fit my budget. Just recently, I may have found the perfect gardener to add to my dream," Roger had said, taking her hand and walking with her further into the building. "I sincerely hope you want to continue gardening," Roger softly spoke as if thinking aloud. "When we finish exploring here, I can show you a quaint café where we can lunch together."

The courtship included Roger sometimes flying back from wherever his work took him to share dinner with her, unique gifts he brought her from his travels and numerous phone calls between them.

After only several months of dating, Roger had proposed to her. When Roger asked her to be his wife, he had shown up unannounced while she was gardening by the tropical waterfalls at the Conservatory. While any residential outdoor gardens had suffered severe damnation under the past several summers of excessive heat, the Conservatory was climate controlled and had remained vibrant, lush, growing, and green. There, after she had searched the garden greenhouses for the most interesting moisture-loving plants and added them as accents by the rock waterfalls, Roger had offered her his mother's engagement ring at the end of her day volunteering.

Roger had said, "When we have to be apart, I cannot stop thinking of you, Clarisse. Our relationship has become so important to me. You are even embedded in my future dreams. Clarisse, please say we can be wed soon." He took her into his arms and lifted her chin, looking deeply into her eyes that were misted in tears. "Such a beautiful look in your amazing blue eyes that within them, I can even see a yes from you," Roger had whispered. He slipped the ring on her finger as tears of joy fell from her eyes.

Clarisse returned to the memory of the moment concerning the civil wedding ceremony. Roger had pulled her closer as she moved away from his embrace to reach for the orchid, hoping to buy additional time to evaluate the situation.

"Clarisse, my love," Roger had whispered to her, "As things settle down during the coming year, we can set a date to pursue our church vows. But a civil ceremony now will allow us to begin living together as one. I must appeal to your good accounting sense. In light of my work compensation arrangement, it makes perfect financial sense. It is my understanding that the company would not consider increasing travel demands upon those who are married and established in a particular location. We could use my lack of paying for my apartment as savings set aside for a home of our own.

They have offered to close the Botanical Gardens for the day of our wedding, which can be before the end of this month, any day of our choice. I can already picture you standing by the waterfall among the ferns and flowers in your beautiful gown. A bridal bouquet with orchids would suit you so well. What can be better than enjoying two weddings instead of one? I know religion is dear to your heart, but I am offering you a very sensible solution. I cannot find it in my heart to ask you to consider living with me without a legal commitment. But my fear of being transferred and separated from you haunts me night and day. It has been difficult to respect your wishes. Waiting for our wedding night for another year is so disheartening for both of us. Will you please find it in your heart to marry me both now and then again?"

Being with Roger had been the only thing that had lifted Clarisse's burden of grief and made her begin to reach for a future. Their relationship had been building so perfectly. The chance of him being transferred away and her being left behind would leave an unbearably painful void in her life. She knew she would drop back into a bottomless pit of depression. Clarisse had weighed the fact that she could gain additional time to earn money for the church fees. She would have her

CPA studies out of the way within a month. It made economic sense not to have Roger paying for a substantial apartment lease when he would not be living there.

Caught up by Roger's tender enthusiasm, Clarisse had melted into his arms and found herself agreeing to the civil ceremony. "I will agree to a civil wedding now as long as we reserve a final date for our wedding at the Basilica next year." Their agreement was sealed with a lingering passionate kiss and celebrated with a bottle of wine.

Roger had been elated. "We can honeymoon later in France, after our church wedding, but we have to choose a date next year that will allow us to plan properly for the best seasonal timing for our honeymoon. Wait and see. You will love France, and it will likely be hard for you to leave." Over dinner that night, Roger had opened up a conversation concerning his church records. "I should admit to some difficulty with my church records. The church records of my baptism are in Canada. I need time to obtain the records and whatever the priest finds necessary to give him. I was baptized at a small church that burned down years ago. I have several trips coming up for work in Canada, and I will track my religious records down from either the bishop's office or perhaps from my old school records if need be. Obtaining the old records requires that I go there in person. I should admit to you that with all my activity at work, I had even been mistaken concerning the date we had set to meet with the priest. I was astonished to walk in your door and find the priest sitting in the kitchen. I assumed that he was likely ready to ask for documents that I did not have in hand at the moment."

Roger's tender pleas and the simple solution had swept away her notion of waiting for a church wedding. Roger had won over Clarisse's heart concerning the matter. But as the month progressed, his schedule had kept shifting until it only allowed him a particular Friday off, which gave them three days to have their civil wedding and remain undisturbed together. Clarisse could not recall anything negative between them that occurred before the wedding. They both had hurried along doing everything required for the civil wedding ceremony.

Clarisse spotted a quick gas shop and purchased a couple of protein bars in case her appointment was longer than her breakfast. She also remembered to pick up an available employment publication. That being done, her thoughts turned back to their wedding planning.

CHAPTER FIVE

After Roger had proposed, Clarisse had felt energized, and due to all the excitement, all traces of her depression had withered away. Her friend Mary could hardly wait to tell her about a wedding dress she had seen displayed, which she said she knew Clarisse would fall in love with. They had gone to the bridal shop together and proved Mary's opinion accurate. The gown was slim, sleeveless, and perfectly tailored, with a delicate lace panel in the front from the scooped neckline to the floor. It was a perfect fit for Clarisse and needed no adjustments. The satin bow on the back of the waist trailed to the bottom of the dress. The veil was simple, trimmed in lace, and not intended to cover her face. The dress could be left at the store, pre-pressed, and picked up just before the wedding.

When Clarisse was ready to pay for her dress, Mary had surprised her. "My Aunt owns this store. It is agreed as our wedding present to you, the friends and the family discount will be applied to the price of your gown and veil." Clarisse had hugged Mary and thanked her profusely. It turned out to be a hefty savings of nearly five hundred dollars on the cost of the gown and veil.

"The dress is perfect. It won't get tangled up in the greenery or florals by the waterfalls," Mary had said with a smile. "I help out working at the shop here sometimes, which is how I saw the perfect dress so you can be the most beautiful bride Buffalo has ever seen."

"Mary," Clarisse had said, "is it possible for you to be my bridesmaid?" One look at Mary confirmed the answer was yes.

The wedding plans had fallen into place at a rapid breakneck pace. After he proposed, Roger had ordered the custom-made wedding bands from a private jeweler. The bands were already waiting for pickup. Roger already owned a tuxedo. Clarisse planned the layout around the waterfalls for the wedding. She had sketched out her plan when the head of the horticulture department approached her and asked to see Clarisse's design.

"This plan is far too plain and simple," her supervisor had remarked. "This is an exciting and significant event for us, or we would not be closing the conservatory for the day. We have never had the opportunity or pleasure to meet our major donors face-to-face until this special occasion. Our team is planning to move a lot of specimens around and even relocate the largest ferns and palms into the conference area. Roger's employer has decided to pay for a reception and photographer for your wedding. Please take the list with a selection of the menu choices. In the next day or two, please give us a head count of the guests you expect and their meal selections. The

Conservatory considers this an extraordinary event. Please include the entire Board of Directors on your guest list and the heads of all our departments. Here are their names and a large box of invitations. We can deliver all the Conservatory-related invitations if you fill them out. In the interest of saving time, we have indicated their meal choices. The Donors are bringing their promotional photographer to be used for the occasion at no charge to you. Be prepared for a lot of picture-taking. Here is the name and number of a hair stylist to get you looking top-notch for your wedding day. It is my understanding that it is prepaid for you also. Dust off the peat moss and start getting ready for your starring role. Your wedding here will be a notable Buffalo event published in a spread in the Buffalo Sunday News and Spree magazine."

Clarisse had never supposed the Botanical Garden would go to such measures. Their plan was outstandingly beautiful. The catering firm was one of the top-rated in Buffalo, NY. Clarisse and Roger had no family to invite. She invited a few coworkers from the audit firm she worked at and several volunteers from the conservatory. Roger had explained he had no co-workers in the Buffalo area, had left his college relationships behind, and that most of his other co-workers were attending a conference he was excused from attending. Clarisse valued meeting the entire Board of Directors and whomever Northwest Pharmaceutical sent to participate in the occasion. After the invitations, all that was left to do was obtain the wedding license and pick up her gown, Roger's tux at the cleaners, and the wedding bands. Roger worked out of town for most of the month before the wedding.

Clarisse had never actually glimpsed Roger's passport until the day that he had used it for a second form of identification for their wedding license. The name on his passport was Rogerio Baudelaire, not Roger Baudelaire. When he took it out of his briefcase and handed it to the clerk, she had remarked, "You, Sir, are an incredibly profuse world traveler." Roger had stiffened. As soon as the clerk handed back the passport, Roger had quickly slipped it into his briefcase. The lock on his briefcase had snapped with such crisp finality that it echoed in the relatively barren office. In response to her query, as they had driven away, Roger casually mentioned to Clarisse that everyone who knew him usually used the Americanized first name, Roger. Clarisse had noticed a second passport when his briefcase briefly opened, but she had assumed it was an expired prior passport. Most people kept their old passports.

Mary was a wedding witness for Clarisse, and they had spent the pre-wedding night at Clarisse's apartment sharing take-out food and a bottle of wine. It was a hurried but joyful morning. The ceremony was scheduled for mid-day, but they were expected for a lengthy trip to the hair salon exceedingly early. The hairstylist would be noted in the news coverage, so she excessively fussed over the girl's hair and the application of cosmetics. She decided to travel to the wedding site in the limo with the two girls to ensure that every hair was in place and their makeup was perfect for the lighting and the photos.

Forboding clouds had gathered by the time Mary and Clarisse were dressed and picked up by the limo and taken to the Buffalo Conservatory. Mary's Aunt had made an artful choice of a dress for Mary. Once her Aunt had worked some magic with her alterations, Mary had looked scarcely pregnant and perfectly lovely. Dressed and ready, Clarisse was the picture of a truly stunning bride. As she gave herself a final look in the mirror, she had been transformed into a vision of perfection. Clarisse could not recall anything amiss between Roger and herself during the hectic wedding preparations.

Clarisse continued to reflect upon the wedding day. Upon arrival, at one glance against the darkening sky, it was impossible for Clarisse to ignore that the management of the Conservatory had turned the building into a backdrop awaiting a Cinderella and a Prince. The immense high domes of the conservatory glowed blue against the darkening sky. A red carpet had graced the entry. Clarisse noticed that the twinkling warm golden lights, lit in every conceivable place, immediately changed the everyday mood inside the Conservatory. Mary and Clarisse were immediately ushered into a side room so Roger would not see his bride until she entered the arranged ceremony setting. A siege of heat lightening began creating unique fleeting shadows near the tall palms, but the storm generated no rainfall.

The only moments before the ceremony that had seemed unusual to Clarisse occurred when the three donors came to the side room with the photographer and her interchanges with them. The door to the room had suddenly swung open. Three tuxedoed men stood in the doorway. Behind them, Clarisse could see the heat lightening raging outside and lighting up the blue high glass dome of the conservatory. A sudden cold draft swept into the room. The smallest of the men, obviously in charge of the situation, had approached her and introduced himself as Satordi Jourdain. He had indicated that the two others were Alexandre Chapelle and Gervais Carbonneau. Clarisse had immediately disliked how the three Northwest Pharmaceuticals donors meticulously and carefully scrutinized her. Satordi Jourdain then announced to Clarisse that they had requested that they have several group photos with the bride. He mentioned the photos would substantiate their charity activity with the Conservatory as donors, which put Clarisse at a fraction of ease but did not alleviate the pangs of wariness suspended in her stomach. Satordi's shriveled and leathery face wore thick-lensed glasses through which he constantly squinted until his eyes remained contorted into slits and lost within his facial skin. It was impossible to look him directly in the eye. Clarisse felt repelled by his deceptive way of whispering when he spoke.

After the photographer had taken several group photographs, Satordi Jourdain had remained beside Clarisse. "I must have a photo alone with this exquisite bride," Satordi said. He sidled closer to Clarisse and whispered to her, "Rogerio told us that when he found you, he found the fairest of all flowers here at the Conservatory. He described your beauty, but I can see now that his words fell short of your innocent, pure radiance." Then, Satordi had slipped his boney hand around her waist for the photograph. Clarisse had jumped slightly and shuttered at his icy cold touch. "I guess I should have warned you about my extremely low blood pressure. They are waiting in New Jersey and France to receive a photo and share how lucky our Rogerio is today," Satordi said with an underlying excuse for a smile. After the photograph was taken, Satordi whispered,

"Our Rogerio shared with me that you are still a virgin." Clarisse had taken a quick breath in response to his remark. She could scarcely believe Roger would discuss something so personal with his employer or anyone else. Satordi continued, "I do not mean to offend you, my dear. It was intended as a complement. It is remarkable in this day and age and a precious scarce gift to bring to a wedding night." Clarisse had sighed in relief when the conversation was interrupted by the Botanical Garden Board of Directors bursting into the room and asking for a group photograph with Clarisse.

After all her years of volunteering, it had seemed fitting that her favorite Conservatory Board member had volunteered to walk Clarisse down the aisle to the waterfalls. Another Board Member had offered to play violin for the walk to the waterfall and the couple's departure from the waterfall. The staff at the Conservatory were all used to seeing the peat-dusted version of Clarisse. But for this occasion, she had bloomed into a breathtakingly radiant sight that outpaced the beauty of her bouquet of rare fresh orchids.

CHAPTER SIX

T he conservatory clock had struck twelve when Clarisse emerged from the side room to the sweet strains of the violin as the Conservatory Board Director escorted her down the pathway to the waterfalls. The warm smell of greenery, cinnamon ferns, and moss complimented the fresh scent of the water cascading over the rock waterfall. Reflections from the clustered blinking, small warm golden lights had continually danced upon her wedding gown as she gracefully stepped towards the Justice of the Peace, where Roger awaited her. He had a look of entrancement upon his face as Clarisse's escort placed her hand in Roger's.

"My beautiful Princess," Roger had whispered and then caught his breath. Amidst the magical setting, Clarisse had looked up at Roger with tears in her eyes. Lost in the moment, Roger had leaned forward to kiss Clarisse.

Justice La Cour had quickly wedged his book of vows between them. "No. No. We must make the vows first. Always vows must come first," the Justice had intercepted.

Soft laughter had cascaded from the onlookers. The Justice had checked his watch and quickly finished the ceremony. The Justice's words were lost due to the severe thunder and lightning that lit the conservatory. But by the time the Justice motioned to Roger that he may kiss the bride, Roger and Clarisse were already lost in an embrace and engulfed in a long lingering kiss. It was the most heartfelt kiss they had ever shared, and it had spoken to Clarisse of the beautiful new life before them.

There had been a sudden urgent tug at Roger's sleeve just as the kiss was winding down. Satordi Jourdain then interrupted by saying, "Come along now. We must stay on schedule. My jet engines are running." Abruptly woken back to reality, Clarisse and Roger had then briskly departed down a rice-pelted pathway.

Clarisse recalled the reception; nothing was amiss as far as Roger was concerned. She had noticed that Roger always maintained formality in front of the Northwest individuals. Satordi had witnessed for Roger, so he sat at Roger's side during the meal. Roger was left-handed, while Clarisse was right-handed, allowing them to periodically and discreetly hold hands under the table.

There was another unusual incident that Clarisse could recall. When the champagne was served, Satordi Jourdain had insisted that he give the toast to the bride and groom. "We wish much good fortune to Rogerio and Clarisse Baudelaire. May this event be the beginning of a future that forever changes all of our lives." Clarisse thought his words were odd, but by that time, there was no doubt in Clarisse's mind that Satordi was a highly unusual man.

After the ceremony and early afternoon reception, after much congratulations, the two of them had returned to Clarisse's apartment under a foreboding sky. Clarisse had felt so beautiful in her wedding dress, deeply in love and yet intensely shy about losing her innocence. Roger had sung French songs to her as he opened a bottle of wine.

"Finally, my love, we can be together," Roger had said. "It's so dark it has moved the afternoon into the evening light." He had then lit the mulberry-scented candles on the coffee table. "This scent reminds me of New Orleans. It's an interesting place. Some good memories and some moments that I insist on forgetting," he had commented.

"Have you slept with a lot of women?" Clarisse had curiously asked.

Roger had laughed at her question. "Only enough to convince me to stay single. I should have waited for you, but as some say, boys will be boys."

"I do have another question," Clarisse had said. "How did you come to mention to Satordi that I was still a virgin?"

Roger looked at her with a surprised look written on his face. "I never discussed any such thing with him. Did he tell you that I did?"

"Yes, strangely enough, he did," Clarisse answered.

"You have to trust me on this one. Satordi is a unique creature. I am sorry if he upset you; he likely only said that to see your response. I would have no reason to discuss our relationship with him," Roger had responded.

"I believe you. It was just such an outlandish remark that it stunned me," Clarisse had replied. "It's our wedding night, and we both need to escape from his grasp."

"Amen," Roger had whispered.

"I do feel inexperienced. I guess you will lead, and I will follow along," Clarisse had replied.

"That sounds like a perfect plan," Roger had replied.

Roger had then led her into the bedroom, where he gently coaxed her out of her wedding dress, reminding her she would get to wear it again for their second wedding. "It seems there is a lot of complicated gift wrap with a princess hidden somewhere inside," Roger had mused as he helped her out of her dress. Heat lightning lit up the room just as Clarisse finally stood naked before him. "So beautiful, so beautiful," Roger had murmured. He slipped off his shirt and then pulled her close against him. The touch of Roger's bare skin melded against her had lent their kiss a passion previously unknown by Clarisse. Roger then moved closer to back Clarisse to the bed that awaited them both.

Suddenly, Roger's cell phone had beeped, indicating a waiting text message. He had picked up his phone, promising to turn it off, but then confusion flooded his face. An auto had yielded a quick beep outside the apartment, and Roger moved the lace shade to look out of the bedroom window. A cold chill had swept by them both. "Get under the covers. I need to clarify what three days of privacy actually means," Roger had sighed in exasperation. He threw his shirt back on.

After Roger had left the apartment, Clarisse slipped into her robe and silently moved over near the window to see what had caught Roger's interest. A black limo had parked in front of the apartment. The driver had rolled down the passenger window as Roger approached. Clarisse had watched as the confrontation became increasingly animated. Roger had started to defuse himself from the conversation and walk away, but the passenger called Roger back. As the passenger had stepped out of the limo and lightning flashed, Clarisse recognized Satordi's glasses in the illuminated light. Roger had taken several sheets of paper from Satordi and read them in the lighting that the driver offered when he opened the front door to the limo. Roger had seemed to hesitate when asked to sign, but after Satordi added some information to the document, Satordi and Roger eventually signed the papers. Satordi took a large envelope out of the back seat and slammed it down on the limo's hood. After a few more words had been exchanged between them, Roger took possession of the envelope and walked away to return to the apartment. Clarisse had slipped back into bed by the time Roger reentered the apartment.

Roger had then appeared at the bedroom door with the envelope and his briefcases. "Surprises never cease," He had said in an agitated state. "I have to leave for France for two weeks. It seems they rewrote my contract and want to install me to my higher-level position immediately."

Clarisse had gotten out of bed, thrown on her robe, and run over to him. "Now? You have to leave, now? Now, on our wedding night?" she asked.

"What wedding night?" Roger said. "The marriage license could not be filed appropriately because Justice La Cour is only authorized in New Jersey. Satordi claims they will straighten matters out because they don't want to be embarrassed due to all the publicity over our wedding. He made no apology that he rescheduled everything today." Roger had slipped his arms inside her robe and held her close. Clarisse had felt something hard and cold against her bare breast and moved back. "It's just the fountain pen in my shirt pocket," Roger remarked.

Clarisse was crestfallen and stunned by the news that Roger was leaving. Roger had then pulled himself away from her. "I am too angry to discuss this further right now. We will see what transpires over the next weeks. That should give them plenty of time to fix the situation. As always, I have my suitcase packed in my car. They are waiting for me," he had said. The limo horn broke the silence with its quick sharp beep. "They are getting impatient, and I must leave now. I had no idea this would happen." That being said, Roger quickly left the apartment.

Clarisse had sat down on the bed, unable to control an onslaught of unstoppable tears as the limo pulled away from the curb. Sleep had evaded her that night. Clarisse had thought the night would end with her falling asleep engulfed in the warmth of Roger's arms, feeling complete at long last and basking in the glow of the prospect of their continuing love and life together. Her wedding day had tumbled from heights of celebration and elation into a damningly dismal abyss. Her last thought before falling asleep had been that this was her punishment for trying to take a shortcut to her church wedding.

Just as the morning crested, Clarisse had awakened to realize she had finally dozed off for two hours. She also realized Roger's leaving last night was a stark reality. Clarisse had headed into the bathroom and threw cold water on her face. She had chided herself, thinking that maybe if she had only tried to stop him from leaving, he would have stayed. But Clarisse had also begun to suspect that Roger might be a workaholic locked in a vice grip concerning his employment. She had been aware of his long hours of work and the additional preparation time involved with his work, even during his off hours. Clarisse had thought that in time, with her overflowing love and devotion, Roger would change. She had assumed that once they were married and living together, she could bring the needed balance into his life, but the hopeless part was that there was no way to control the work demands put on him. The thought that perhaps Satordi had some control over Roger that reached beyond a working relationship occurred to her, but it seemed like a far-fetched idea. Likely, Roger was vying for a contract with Northwest and perhaps not an employee but in a contract relationship. Either way, knowing she was pitted against the demands and commands of Satordi Jourdain wasn't going to lend towards even footing. If she had to fight for her future life with Roger, Clarisse found her gentle ways made her ill-equipped for an ongoing battle.

CHAPTER SEVEN

Lost in thought, as she walked the six blocks, Clarisse stumbled slightly over an uneven edge on the sidewalk and then continued to sift through her situation with Roger. She wished his shortfalls were as expected, such as leaving his shoes in front of the door or wet towels on the floor in the bathroom. Clarisse had to admit that Roger had increasingly become nothing short of a puzzle to her.

After two weeks following their wedding, Roger had returned but offered no detailed explanations about the disappointing wedding night except that the filing of the license matter was still unresolved. He had returned tired, irritable, unenthused, and distant. He had brushed aside her warm welcome home. Roger moved his possessions into her apartment and had quickly converted the second bedroom into a study environment. Afterward, Roger had spent most of his time there, claiming an increased workload.

Clarisse found it frustrating that Roger conversed in French during any calls he made or received. After she had disturbed him several times by bringing him coffee while he was working, he began to lock the door, so she would not disrupt him. It irritated Clarisse that Roger had been so intent on taking such lengths to maintain privacy from her, but she was patient and passed by any slim opportunity to address it with him. Clarisse knew Roger was accustomed to living alone. His work seemed never-ending because he was at Satordi's beck and call, which included the need for overseas calls during the early morning and the late night hours. She hoped things would ease up as he got used to being married. But she also reasoned that his work habits were well-established before they married, and she might have to accept that. Roger was either vying for a large bonus or the coveted title of Workaholic of the Year.

Roger seemed to have arrived into her life from a hazy somewhere and went to work at scantily shared locations. Much of Roger's past and current daily life remained a mystery to Clarisse and one she began to make an effort to resolve. When Clarisse finally brought herself to try to find traces of Roger's past on the internet, it appeared neither a Roger nor a Rogerio Baudelaire existed. Roger had a passport, so perhaps he had a name change, was all she could suppose. She was waiting for an opportune moment to ask about it, but so far, no opportunity had arrived. At the onset of the slightest question, Roger had stonewalled her by immediately recalling that he had work to do, going into his study, and then closing and locking the door.

With Roger traveling for work the majority of the time and being called out of town on short notice, it had become increasingly easy for Roger to avoid conversation. If and when they were both at home during the day, he simply further immersed himself in his work, alone in the study. Any meaningful discussion had become as elusive as campfire smoke in the wind. Roger had become so possessive of the room they called the study that he had resorted to dusting and vacuuming the room himself. Thus there was no need for her to have any access whatsoever to his study.

Roger had never given her any office phone numbers, claiming he was seldom, if ever, required actually to be in the New Jersey home office. When three of his superiors from work had appeared at the wedding, they had seemed to be formal and distant enough to make Clarisse uncomfortable. They had managed to turn a personal event into a gala for their purposes, where she was featured as window dressing. Beneath their cordial surface, Clarisse had felt an icy edge of cold calculation about them.

If needed during the day, Clarisse always called Roger on his cell phone, which was also the only telephone number listed on his business card. Now that they were married, it was more likely that she found herself leaving him a message and awaiting a return call that remained unanswered.

Roger had never discussed his work or described his job in any detail. His business card stated that he was Chief Medical Advisor for Northwest Pharmaceuticals, but after web searching, Clarisse found that the company had no website. Clarisse supposed the company was part of a conglomerate, but it still seemed odd no references appeared on the first 20 pages of her search. According to what Roger told her when they were dating, his employment travel requirements had spanned the continental US, Canada, Mexico, and France was involved somehow. Roger was also sent on various other European job assignments. Clarisse had finally arrived at the point of admitting that they surely had rushed into matrimony at maximum speed. Yes, indeed. To date, Roger had not allowed her to inquire about anything.

Before their wedding, Clarisse had assumed that Roger had ample earnings, although they never directly discussed it. He had brought her thoughtful, high-end gifts from his trips abroad. Looking back on matters, Clarisse had supposed that his expensive Lexus and how Roger dressed had helped create that impression. Even if it was his mother's ring, Roger had given Clarisse an engagement ring set with a substantial diamond. He had ordered expensive wedding bands custom-made by a private jeweler. But after the wedding, Clarisse had finally discovered Roger had few possessions of his own. Merging their households had been surprisingly simple. Roger had been living in furnished corporate apartments since college and had acquired few items. That made sense to Clarisse.

Although she had felt a certain amount of guilt, rather than attempting to ask Roger about the Lexus, she had opted to slip into the car in the middle of the night and rifle the Lexus' glove box. He had set his car keys down on the kitchen counter before supper. When he received a phone call and stepped into the hall for his conversation, Clarisse concealed the keys behind a supper serving dish. Roger had gone to the study none the wiser. She had found the car was a leased vehicle issued to the company that had employed him since the year before they met. He had never mentioned not owning or owning the auto. Clarisse had concluded she should have simply asked him about the ownership, but Roger now seemed short with her over trivial questions. It appeared that Roger only personally owned his expensive, extensive wardrobe, several locked leather attaché cases, a substantial number of locked file cabinets, leather luggage, bookshelves, and an overwhelming library of medical books.

Clarisse had assumed, once they married, that things would follow the usual vein of a joint household bank account and planning for their financial future, but to date, she had never seen a Northwest payroll stub. She still did not even have any inkling exactly where Roger banked. He had explained to her his briefcase, cell phone, and laptop computer must remain locked due to office protocol. Roger was meticulous about locking all his personal information in his briefcase, which he kept in the study or with him at work. Clarisse logically felt this was due to his being used to traveling and ensuring he did not mislay anything. Some of his work assignments resulted from emergency phone calls. Roger remained packed with his suitcase in his car and ready to leave on their corporate jet immediately. There was no opportunity to find clues in his pockets while doing laundry. Roger sent his laundry and dry cleaning out to be done and picked it up himself.

After the wedding, Clarisse had suggested they alternate paying the household expenses. Roger had made it abruptly clear that he expected her to continue to pay for the apartment, which they now shared, and all the rest of the household expenses. Roger expected her to use her funds and account. He claimed he was saving his money to purchase a home as soon as possible. She had wanted to discuss it with him, but he seemed to instinctively know how to avoid discussing any finances. From an accounting standpoint, there was no way that Clarisse would agree to sign any blank tax returns. Clarisse had set the sensitive issue concerning his income aside. She had hoped the vagueness of the situation would unravel itself out of necessity at income tax time. However, Roger had recently expressed he intended to file separately. Clarisse now felt grateful about not having a joint return.

What had become excruciatingly painful for Clarisse was that, somehow, wedded bliss had fizzled out on their wedding night. Roger's employer had critically disrupted Roger from bedding her by showing up outside their apartment and having a heated discussion with Roger over paperwork he insisted Roger sign. It almost seemed like Satordi was letting her know from the get-go that she was second place in Roger's life. Roger was forced into a choice that night, and he left with Satordi for several weeks in France. Now Roger was either traveling for work or retreating to his study, locking the door and shutting her out without explanation. Since the wedding night, he was heavily rejecting her attachment to him, which had caused an uncomfortable pause between them.

Despite her increasing disappointment, Clarisse had made every effort to examine things objectively. During the past weeks since their wedding, they had spent their time alone rather than together. Roger had spent most of his work week traveling. When they were at home together, Roger seemed deeply preoccupied and refused to be interrupted while he worked long into the night. If the conversation was not kept casual at supper, Roger shortened his mealtime.

Clarisse spent her late evenings reading or studying while she faithfully waited up for Roger but to no avail. They had married so that he did not have to be apart from her, yet he created a tremendous distance between them within the walls of their apartment. At the moment, he seemed put out with her that her employment had folded, but it seemed just another excuse to avoid any trace of intimacy.

Clarisse had to admit that she was at her wit's end concerning moving forward in the situation. Continuing to be locked in the current confines of the relationship was too painful and confusing. The more space she gave Roger, the more space he took. Clarisse needed to talk to someone with a more rounded view of relationships than Farther David, but she was drawing a blank in that department.

CHAPTER EIGHT

Clarisse turned the corner into the street where the clinical evaluation was scheduled according to the letter. She double-checked the address. It appeared odd that the clinic was located in an older, nondescript two-story house rather than a professional office building. Clarisse had expected a long line of applicants, so she had arrived a full hour earlier than her scheduled appointment. The situation outside the building showed no hub of activity at all.

When she entered the main door, a mild dose of weak, cooler air attempted to revive her as she stood facing a drab, deserted hallway. It was apparent the house had been converted into offices at some point. The smell of old dust clung to the hall carpet. To all appearances, the building lacked previous use for some time. Limp pieces of paper dangled from tape on the interior hall doors. Each of those doors displayed a different pencil-written project number. It was certainly not what Clarisse had expected, but with the amount of money offered to the participants, she supposed they had to cut corners in some fashion. She could always refuse to participate if something about the project appeared suspicious. Door 6 matched the project identification numbers on her letter.

The interior door emitted a loud creak when she opened it. The office was definitely a temporary situation. The room was barren except for a stack of applicant packets and a sheet of instructions on the table. After completion, the application was to be deposited into the narrow slit near the privacy glass sliding window. Five women in their mid-twenties to perhaps thirty years of age sat at a large table in the center of the room. The only sound piercing the silence was the turning of the applicant's pages as they remained engrossed in completing their applications. Clarisse picked up an application packet, took the last seat available at the table, and began filling out what seemed to be endless pages of information. The first page only asked for standard basic details, which Clarisse handled quickly.

An outgoing, well-dressed woman was seated next to her. The woman glanced her way and whispered, "Hi. Do you know or have any idea what this project is all about?"

Clarisse smiled and shrugged her shoulders. "I guess we'll find out when they decide to tell us."

Clarisse immediately felt devoid of any shred of a current fashion sense while seated next to the woman. Clarisse always contrived her wardrobe to be conservative and tailored. It was her habit to be critical of women who made it a point to follow current trends. She had found, time and again, that those who find it necessary to dress as fashion dictates seldom have much to offer beyond their visual appeal. But she noticed an underlying beauty radiated from this particular woman, who looked closer to thirty than Clarisse. The woman could have been dressed poorly, and she still would have looked stunning. On second glance, Clarisse softened her opinion. The fashion trends were actually understated. It was the fabric of her clothes that looked expensive. Clarisse's eye was drawn to the woman's denim jeans. They were distinctive and tastefully detailed with leather.

The woman caught Clarisse's glance. "I'm sorry," she said. "I noticed what you wrote on your first page and was pretty surprised. I saw the fabulous wedding spread in the Buffalo Sunday edition a few weeks ago. I work in advertising, and those were some outstanding and beautiful photos of you. Seeing the news article, I noticed that our last names are exactly the same." The woman flipped her application back to the first page, revealing her name as Marcie Michel-Laurent.

"It's not a common last name," Clarisse mused and shook her head. "At the moment, I certainly feel dressed like a Cinderella. I walked here, and it was so hot outside." Marcie and Clarisse shared low-key laughter.

"You are so right about this un-Godly heat. But what are the chances of two, Michel-Laurent's, applying for the same thing?" When Marcie commented, it caught the attention of the four other women at the table.

"Did you mention the name Laurent?" A woman across from Marcie asked while she showed the others the first page of her application.

"Are we all sharing the same last name?" she asked. "Perhaps the letters that they sent out were issued alphabetically?"

"The two of us are Michel-Laurent, not just Laurent," Marcie clarified to the other applicants. Marcie then turned to Clarisse, "This is an unexpected opportunity to discover if we are related in some way. Could you perhaps flip over to page five, Clarisse?"

Clarisse looked at the page in question. It requested parentage and family genealogical history as far back as one could recall. Odd, she thought but proceeded to fill in as many as possible, which was six generations. Marcie watched with interest.

"I still cling to using my maiden name," Clarisse ventured. "I'm on top of this question. I researched it in depth last year. I was so interested in my roots that I even purchased a DNA test kit and sent it to be processed.

A quick comparison showed that Marcie and Clarisse shared a common strand, dating back prior to their families immigrating to America.

Marcie issued a friendly smile. "Hurry up and fill out the rest. Wait until you see some of the insane questions. Maybe we can take time to chat while we wait for the interview. I'm curious about what you know concerning the family history back then. If you don't mind me asking, did anything interesting unfold from your DNA report?"

"I'm still waiting on the DNA findings," Clarisse responded. "They've taken enough time to trace my ancestry back to Adam and Eve. I keep calling them, but all the answer I get is that these things take time. I told them I was not impressed considering how slow their work has been compared to how much they charged me and how fast they processed my charge card."

"I hear you," Marcie commented. "Life is more take than give when it comes to money these days."

Two of the women pushed their paperwork into the slot, and immediately the window opened by several scant inches. Behind the sliding window, the first name of one of the women was called. After fifteen minutes, the woman exited the inner office with a confused look. Through the slit in the sliding glass, the second woman was called into the inner office.

The woman, who had been rejected for the testing, walked over to Marcie and confidentially enlightened her. "They gave me fifty bucks for coming and told me Laurent needed to be my maiden name. I had to fill out what I knew about my husband's family, which isn't much since I'm newly married." She shrugged and left, saying, "Fifty bucks is fifty bucks, but I gave up a day's pay to come here."

After the woman had departed, Marcie confided to Clarisse, "Now we are down to only redheads. At least, we know we are each good for a gain of at least fifty bucks."

"Sounds better than nothing at all," Clarisse responded while beginning to warm to Marcie's personality.

Once their applications were completed, Clarisse and Marcie discussed the dates of their family's immigration to America and the history of France at the time. It was forty-five minutes before the next candidate was called and the preceding one excused.

The next prospective candidate emerged from the exit door of the inner office.

"What happened?" Marcie asked, with her easygoing, take-charge attitude.

"Something in my medical history, I think," the woman answered. "I had a car accident some years ago that resulted in several transfusions. That seemed to slam the door of opportunity for me, but they did give me a check for two hundred dollars."

"My, my, the stakes have risen," quipped Marcie with a smile. "We have exceeded the gross wages I lost today to come here."

Clarisse was fascinated by how strangers were immediately at ease with Marcie. Roger had that ability. During a stroll in the park or dinner in a restaurant, Roger could draw unfamiliar individuals out with that same effortless charisma. He could manage to extract incredible amounts of information from strangers. Clarisse often wondered whether it was an acquired ability or a gift with which one was born. She, herself, was incredibly shy and always had been.

Marcie and Clarisse had narrowed down the fact that Clarisse was the descendant of an older brother, overlooked in the details of Marcie's family tree. Clarisse's extensive research found that the family's eldest brother had been, for unknown reasons, raised at Ferme de Tayac, which was at the time functioning as a monastery near Saint Martin's Church in Southern France. Although they lived nearby, he had been separated from his family for some reason. Marcie was one of his natural brother's descendants. While Clarisse's information only listed the related brother, who had lived at the monastery, she did have reliable records of his being a sibling in Marcie's generational family. They decided to research further and exchanged phone numbers because it piqued their curiosity.

Marcie was not married and claimed she enjoyed plenty of free time and could come to see Clarisse at her convenience. Clarisse confessed she was currently unemployed and studying for her CPA exam. They agreed to pursue their research before Clarisse found another job, and their schedules became more complex.

Two more applicants were rejected. One by one, they left with a shrug but also a check in hand.

Marcie was called in next, leaving Clarisse to wait alone as the last to apply. Her watch slowly ticked onward while she stubbornly studied the want ads, searching for a possibility concerning new employment. Finding no likely matches in her area of expertise, Clarisse began mentally sorting through the family history information, hoping for a new lead to provide Marcie. If they could find the year that Marcie's relation came to America, they might also discover other cousins or siblings arriving around that time.

Clarisse decided it might be worth a trip to the local Mormon historical library. The Mormons kept many old lists of passengers on various ships. They opened their library to the public on posted dates. The Mormon library had information on the brother that Clarisse was related to; therefore, Marcie's relation information was also likely to be there. It intrigued Clarisse that they both could spend some time and likely discover living relations they never knew either of them had. The more Clarisse thought about the vast historical data bank the Mormons maintained in Utah concerning US residents, the more she became enthralled at finding distant family members with which they could possibly communicate. Her curiosity was rekindled concerning the separation of her relative and why he ended up living at the monastery rather than at his family home nearby.

It was a full hour before Clarisse's name was called. She expected Marcie would have come out of the exit door by now. She hoped to at least attempt to set up when she and Marcie could meet again, but the exit door remained motionless.

CHAPTER NINE

In a stiffly starched white lab coat, a dark-haired, slender woman sat down with Clarisse to review her information. The woman was obviously of French descent, judging by her heavy accent. She seemed aloof to the point of extreme superiority. Clarisse idly wondered if some of the faults she found with the more formal, reserved attitude Roger had been exhibiting were ill-founded and simply an essential French trait.

Clarisse glanced at the woman's identification badge. She immediately found herself annoyed that the woman wore a photo badge from a testing company, but her name was not affixed for accurate identification. Clarisse had given the woman an application that demanded that she give insight into every corner of her personal life. In contrast, the woman reading the information did not offer her as much as a proper name in exchange. The lack of detail irked Clarisse. Clarisse was a stickler for details. The trait was ingrained in her, and details had been lacking lately. In Clarisse's accounting world, everything was cross footed and balanced to the penny.

Additional history was taken, which further detailed any minor medical incidents. The interviewer specifically asked about any history of transfusions and focused on questions concerning living relatives. Nothing in Clarisse's medical history would have warranted any transfusions. Clarisse's application already stated her parents were deceased. She had no siblings, no children, and had not experienced any miscarriages. The woman's questions seemed redundant. When inquiries were made concerning her husband, Clarisse explained that she had known Roger only two months before their wedding, nearly a month ago. The fact that Roger was born in Canada, had no siblings, and his parents were deceased was all of the information she had to offer. Clarisse was suddenly embarrassed to realize that she didn't know the proper spelling of Roger's parents' first names or his mother's maiden name. She explained that Roger's records were still in Canada and that he would likely obtain them soon.

The interviewer explained to Clarisse, "Submitting to a pregnancy test and having your blood drawn is required for the pretrial examination. If you agree to proceed, you will be given two hundred dollars for the time used to take the two tests. If you decide to take the two tests, the two hundred dollars will be paid to you whether or not you are selected for the trial. If the tests prove satisfactory, you are assured that the project will be further explained, and several more tests of a minor nature will be subject to your consent. At any point, you can decline to become a participant and take the amount of money already promised to you."

Clarisse noticed the time, and as requested in the letter, her cell phone was turned off. "I did not leave a note or explain to my husband where I was going," Clarisse mentioned.

The interviewer firmly advised Clarisse, "It is best if things are kept on schedule. You can call him after the tests, and perhaps you will, by that time, have further news of being accepted as a participant."

Feeling encouraged, Clarisse readily agreed to the testing and to the wait on using her cell phone.

When the lab technician departed after the blood draw, Clarisse caught a glimpse of Marcie passing the doorway in a medical gown. Another technician entered to retrieve her urine sample, and again the door opened momentarily. For a split second, Clarisse thought she heard the sound of Roger's voice. The tests had been immediately administered after she had agreed they could proceed. Clarisse patiently sat there, alone and awaiting the results. She settled into reading a book she had tucked into her purse that morning.

The interviewer returned once again. She explained to Clarisse, "If you agree to a bone density x-ray and a basic internal examination, these two tests will complete the final step. If those tests yield positive results, it will mean acceptance into the clinical trial if you decide to participate. If you elect not to participate, you will receive a total of four hundred dollars for your time."

Clarisse was not about to turn down two hundred additional dollars. She agreed; since she seemed to be moving ever closer to acquiring the coveted amount of fifteen hundred dollars. She gladly accepted a hospital gown. Clarisse was left alone in the room to don the loose fitting gown. She was then escorted into a private examination room.

A technician arrived to administer the bone density scan, which was simple. Clarisse placed her hand inside the small x-ray box, and the scan was completed in seconds. Clarisse was left alone in the examination room to await her internal examination.

Since she had caught a glimpse of Marcie in an examination gown, Clarisse assumed they had both progressed to at least the same acceptance stage. Clarisse was sure that despite internal exams being considered bothersome to most women, Marcie would be in good spirits over the offer of an extra several hundred dollars for giving a doctor a peek into her promised land.

Clarisse had to agree that it would be a first to be paid to endure the exam rather than pay to have an annual check-up. Last year when Clarisse had her scheduled internal exam, the clinic doctor's comment took her aback. The doctor had expressed his surprise that she was still a virgin at age 25. It irked Clarisse that the doctor's remark was broadcasting personal information in front of an assisting nurse.

The nurse had looked at Clarisse and immediately recognized her anger over the remark. The nurse had addressed the doctor. "No one should be surprised if a woman elects to uphold the dictates of her religion concerning premarital sex. Medical records generally note the patient's faith."

Clarisse had then taken the opportunity to chastise the doctor. "If being a virgin makes your job more difficult, I can mention at church that you prefer to examine non-virgins, and use of this medical facility should best be avoided."

The doctor had then glanced over at Clarisse's medical folder and quickly apologized to Clarisse. His excuse was that he had been up all night making several deliveries at the hospital.

After the examination was complete and the doctor departed, the nurse had lingered momentarily. "If medical credentials depended partly upon bedside manner, that particular doctor would have never graduated," the nurse said to Clarisse. "I welcome any opportunity to offset his rather stupid remarks."

CHAPTER TEN

The silence in the room was broken when a nurse and several doctors entered. Not a single word of English was spoken the entire time that Clarisse lay on the table during her examination. The staff had spoken French in the hall before they entered the room and during the entire examination. They seemed distinctly aware that Clarisse had no working knowledge of French and lacked any understanding of their conversations. She tried to ask several questions in English but to no avail. She was swiftly motioned that silence was expected of her.

Clarisse's annoyance began to tick inside her. She tried to excuse the matter by internally suggesting that perhaps it was more efficient for them to speak their native language. But as the examination progressed, she noticed and began to resent their consistently cold, clinical attitudes, which were undoubtedly reflected in the way they physically handled her. She had not been forewarned that any internal tissue sample would be taken, let alone a number of them. Clarisse tried to convince herself that the language barrier was distorting her perceptions concerning the examination. Once again, she was being isolated by a language that had begun to play too dominant a role in her personal life. There was nothing she could do but remind herself that this time she was being compensated for the examination, but the extent of the exam and the time they took baffled her. Her mind idled back to her marital difficulties.

When she first met Roger, he had sung what seemed to be enchanting and endearing romantic songs to her when he stopped to see her while she volunteered at the Conservatory. She was surprised that when he translated them, they were just phrases contrived out of utter nonsense. Clarisse had come to regret that she had limited her language electives in school only to Latin.

Roger had laughed and said, "Anything that sounds romantic is romantic. They were songs my Mother sang to me as a child."

Clarisse mused over whether to ask Roger to teach her some French or take some sort of a computer course. It suddenly seemed odd that Roger had never mentioned that she should learn French. His habit of speaking French on the phone curbed her knowledge of his conversations. The phone calls never seemed casual but rather so medical in nature that she would have been hopelessly lost as to the content. Deep inside, it only nurtured her belief that she was being deliberately limited within their relationship for some reason. Once she brought herself to the point of making that mental accusation, she was left hoping and praying that she was exaggerating the situation.

Marriage was new to both of them. Clarisse admitted to herself that they were in a period of adjusting to living with one another. Perhaps some of her troubling thoughts were ill-founded. It was quite possible her habit of critically overthinking matters was enhancing the difficulty within their relationship. It was also entirely possible Roger was experiencing problems at work. Today's thoughts certainly hadn't done her a world of good. Going home while fostering an attitude was not going to help matters any.

Once the exam was completed and Clarisse had redressed, she crossed the hall to return to the interview area. She was a bit unnerved by a few fleeting French syllables that drifted out from behind one of the closed doors. It sounded like Roger's voice, but Clarisse brushed the thought away and sat back down to wait for the results of the tests.

The interviewer and the examination doctor seemed more relaxed and agreeable when they explained the study to her. The trial would be based on generational comparisons of blood, bone density, cholesterol, DNA variations, and allergy similarities, of those with heritage, from a particular region in France. To ensure accurate results, a critical time frame was needed to accomplish the clinical trial. Clarisse was assured that the clinical tests were painless and far less intense than those she had just experienced. But it was deemed necessary that the participants be gathered in a single location to complete the study efficiently and within a controlled environment. All travel, accommodations, and food would be fully paid for. The study was to be accomplished, over a period of one week, at a location in the South of France. If she declined to participate in the study, she would be paid the four hundred dollars promised to her. It was her choice.

Clarisse was pleasantly stunned. Any traces of her initial annoyance quickly faded. Being unemployed while spending a week in the South of France was an unlikely combination and quite a turn of events. After Clarisse expressed her interest in participating in the study, the interviewer advised her that she would receive Seven Hundred Fifty dollars today. An equal amount would be given to her upon her completion of the test week. Her travel tickets and instructions would arrive by courier. She was encouraged to read the contract and then call her husband. As part of the agreement, they needed to verify that he approved her absence, for a week, with her departure within a matter of days.

Clarisse read through the two-page agreement. She immediately noticed the project was funded by the same pharmaceutical company that employed Roger. For once, when she called Roger on his cell phone, he actually answered his phone.

Clarisse found that Roger was actually delighted over her opportunity and felt a trip abroad might prove to lift her spirits. "Just this morning, I was told that I would be required to leave for France to attend a conference in Paris," he said. "I will know further details by the end of the day." When she told Roger that his employer funded the study, he told her not to hesitate to take the check and sign on the dotted line. Clarisse was encouraged by how cheerful Roger sounded at her prospect of travel.

The doctor seemed overly confident that she would sign. He offered her the use of his gold nibbed fountain pen even before she was finished discussing it with Roger on the phone. She held the weighty pen in her hand while conversing with Roger. The pen barrel appeared made of garnet with a gold emblem identical to that of Northwest Pharmaceuticals embedded in the side of the stone. On the top of the pen was what appeared to be a family crest. As she curiously studied the impressive pen for a moment, she recognized that the Justice of the Peace at their wedding had used an identical pen to sign their wedding certificate. When Clarisse began to spin the pen in her hand as she spoke, the Doctor quickly retrieved the fountain pen and removed the top section that usually covered the pen nib. He handed the bare pen back to her.

Clarisse signed the contract. The interviewer also signed the contract, and the Doctor witnessed their signatures. Rather than black or blue as one would expect, Clarisse noticed the ink to be a very dark red. She could not determine their names from their signatures, but she was handed the second copy of the agreement and a check from a US bank which seemed sufficient.

As she shook hands with both, she noticed the doctor had no name beneath his photo identification either. The thought crossed her mind that perhaps the staff was only temporarily hired by the testing company. It was late in the afternoon. With the check in hand, Clarisse was more than ready to hurry home and celebrate her upcoming trip. Her rent was due at the end of the month, and the check would cover that and more.

Clarisse had hoped Marcie might have waited for her, but the anteroom was empty. She decided to try calling Marcie during the walk home. Clarisse felt nervous about traveling abroad and attending the trials alone. She hoped that Marcie had also been selected. Clarisse could not imagine Marcie turning away the opportunity if she had passed the testing, but she supposed it would depend if Marcie could manage to get time off from her regular job.

CHAPTER ELEVEN

Clarisse broke free of her typical spirit of reservation and performed a quick dance of joy on the sidewalk in front of the office. She spun around while holding the check as high to the heavens as possible. A sudden burst of laughter came from the parking area on the street. Feeling rather foolish, Clarisse glanced in the direction of the expressed mirth. Marcie was laughing at her as she readied herself to get into her car. With reckless abandon and without looking for any approaching vehicles, Clarisse ran across the street to Marcie's car. A driver backing out of his driveway laid on his horn when Clarisse darted in back of his car.

"I assume you were accepted?" Marcie inquired. They both needed to take several breaths to calm down.

"Yes! They gave me half of the money upfront!" Clarisse replied. "And you?"

"I'll see you there," Marcie said excitedly. "We lucked out better than fifty or two hundred bucks. But wait, there's more. I asked where we were going to stay. Did you ask?"

"No, I didn't think to ask," responded Clarisse.

"Are you ready for this one?" Marcie said. "The old monastery at Ferme de Tayac is a bed and breakfast now. Back to our roots we both go!"

Clarisse's eyes reflected complete disbelief. "That's incredible! Maybe we can do a little research. We're actually going to tread where our ancestors once walked. Going there is positively too good to be true."

"It certainly seems that way," Marcie said. "Are you sure it's going to be OK with your husband?"

"I already called him, and he gave the green light to the trip!" Clarisse answered. "I'm going to run all the way back to the apartment. I have to get on the Internet and see what the place looks like."

"This is just great," Marcie replied. "Let me give you a lift back to your place before you get run over on the way home and ruin all the great times we could share. There's nothing like getting fab pay and meeting a long-lost relative in one swoop. What a deal. What a day!"

Once in the car, they decided to research the weather in France and the kinds of places they wanted to visit. They agreed to pack light enough to bring some regional treasures home with them.

"I already know I want to stop at any available historic French churches," Clarisse mentioned.

"I agree to that," Marcie said. "For me, it's not a religious interest as much as an architectural one. I'm fascinated with old stone buildings. Now that I think about it, a periodic dose of holy water never hurts anyone, and I'm certainly overdue."

"I have no idea what to pack to wear," Clarisse ventured. "I must confess that most of my wardrobe is white blouses and suits because of the nature of my accounting work."

"Problem solved," Marcie said. "I think we're both the same size. If they don't restrict our dress to classic business wear, I have plenty of fashion statements stuffed in my closet. One dresses in the know while single and shopping for a certain class of man. Out of the public eye, you would laugh yourself silly at my laid-back garb. Sometimes you can even catch me in my old roller hockey jersey."

"You played roller hockey?" Clarisse asked curiously.

"Sure. I played during college. It kept my buns like steel. I've redefined myself since, but I wasn't anybody's sweet little sister a few years ago."

"I think I can imagine you doing that," Clarisse said. "You have a lot of spark."

"There is something about the sound of a ripping puck that can drive the kinks out of one's soul. I carried a mean stick, not to mention my slap shot. Anyway," Marcie countered, "once our directives arrive, we can coordinate our packing."

"Thanks so much for offering that," Clarisse said with a bright smile.

"Anything for a relative," Marcie said. "We are newfound family to one another. I can already picture you in some of my scarves, art jewelry, and leather-trimmed jeans. We are going to be two stunning redheads on a tour of France. Not that I wouldn't dress like you and save the money if I were married. I would switch right over to your low-key classic style that only speaks of high quality. Frankly, I'd be saving my money for a home with a white picket fence. I'll borrow from you if it's only a classic business dress that's acceptable.

"In the interest of holding your man and me finding mine, let's add perusing French perfume to our list of things to do. We can likely shop at the French airport for it. That way, it will slide through customs."

Clarisse agreed. She silently considered that it might be worth her time to learn to dress in a more interesting manner. Being newly married was supposed to be the beginning of an adventure through life together. Marcie could undoubtedly be the key to at least learning how to be better equipped and look more appealing to Roger. Clarisse noticed how uplifted she felt when she was sharing time with an outgoing, upbeat personality such as Marcie. If she learned how to be more positive, perhaps Roger would respond in a like manner.

"I can guarantee our trip will be fun," Marcie said as she dropped Clarisse off at her apartment building. "I have vacation time coming, and expense paid surely works for me. The timing is perfect to ask for the time off. I'm willing to bet our trip to France will be life-changing for both of us. At long last, I get to use my French."

"Great. I need a few French lessons myself," Clarisse answered. She could not believe her luck. She now had a family and a chance to learn some French. Clarisse paused, "Did everyone speak French during your examination?"

"During that episode, no one spoke at all," Marcie responded.

Clarisse walked up the front porch steps and took the mail out of the box by the door. She decided that if she was more open to change, the trip could quite possibly give her a new perspective on things. At some point, perhaps after she knew Marcie better, she could discuss some of her confusion and doubts. Clarisse didn't find it easy to cultivate friendships, but this time the basics had fallen into place easily. That seemed a good indication that she should take advantage of the opportunity, share her thoughts, and perhaps glean some advice rather than dwelling on things alone and solving absolutely nothing.

Clarisse looked at the kitchen clock. She would have just enough time to shower, change her clothes, and make a spectacular effort to look really nice by the time Roger arrived home. Clarisse decided to splurge and have a pizza and wings delivered. It had been weeks since she felt as rejuvenated as she did at the moment.

CHAPTER TWELVE

W hen Roger opened the door to their apartment, Clarisse flew into his arms with the check in hand. He staggered backward when attacked by her gushing enthusiasm. He settled her down by suggesting he open a celebration bottle of wine and that the two of them should sit down and discuss her trip. Since she knew precisely where she would be staying, she was anxious to explore the Internet and see what of interest might be located nearby. Clarisse felt enthused that Roger seemed in good spirits and, most of all, that she had captured Roger's full attention. He seemed to be responding to the new positive version of herself that she was projecting.

Roger began the conversation by handing her a glass of wine and sharing some significant news. "Clarisse, because Northwest Pharmaceuticals is funding the study, you will travel on their jet. At the same time, there is a conference in Paris, and I will take the flight to and from France with you. Of course, our expenses will be fully paid for."

Clarisse shared her immediate thought, "It would be perfect if we could extend our trip for a week even if we had to pay for our airfare home. We planned on a honeymoon in France, and expense-wise, we would be halfway there." However, her excitement was cut short.

"My business in France is elsewhere, so I cannot stay overnight with you, and I have work obligations scheduled during the rest of the month. Extending the trip at this time is out of the question," Roger quickly replied.

Clarisse expressed her disappointment as the damper slammed shut on her enthusiasm. "Wishful thinking aside, my new friend Marcie was also an applicant for the medical trial. We have struck upon the beginnings of what appears to be a great friendship."

"This Marcie you speak of, is she also a trial participant?" Roger inquired as he glanced out of the window.

"Yes, and as we discovered, we are both distant cousins. Do you believe it? I have a family. Maybe there are more of us out there too." Clarisse explained their plan to venture out to see the nearby town from which their families had immigrated.

"Then you are not wholly disappointed and quite comfortable with the prospect of spending a week in France?" Roger inquired. He seemed relieved that she was looking forward to the trip.

"I may even return a changed woman. I discovered that Marcie couldn't help but bring out the positive in everything, including me," Clarisse said with a charming smile. "This is all so amazing. I would never have happened into this wonderful adventure if I hadn't lost my job. As soon as I return, I will sign up with a placement agency, but at the moment, it's ideal that I am free to go to France."

"It would seem there is a purpose to everything that happens," Roger commented. "The timing of your trip could not have been planned better."

The pizza and wings arrived. They finished the wine while they sat at the kitchen table and cruised the Internet on Clarisse's laptop. Clarisse devoured all the photos they could find of the Ferme de Tayac Bed and Breakfast and the surrounding areas.

"I better make notes to share with Marcie about all the sites nearby the Ferme. We might not have a lot of free time, so we will have to be prepared to pick and choose. We want to stop at nearby churches, too," Clarisse confided to Roger as she started filling up a page in her notebook. She jotted down various websites she wanted to share with Marcie. It was the most time together that she and Roger had spent since the wedding. Just as Clarisse reached for Roger's hand and was going to suggest they take their further conversation into their bedroom, Roger's attitude abruptly changed.

"The time has gotten away from me," Roger said hurriedly. "I must work for at least four to six hours tonight. It is the time difference overseas that creates such problems. Why don't you look at additional sites and then go on to bed? There is no sense waiting up for me." That being said, he picked up his briefcase and went into the study. He began making a telephone call just before quickly closing the door and locking it. Clarisse felt crestfallen but consoled herself that at least the ice jam between them had been somewhat broken.

The following morning a courier arrived. Clarisse immediately tore open the envelope and found her detailed instructions and two boarding passes for Northwest Pharmaceutical's private corporate jet from the Buffalo airport to Paris, France. A limo would take her from Paris to the Ferme. An airport transport would pick them up and deliver them to the airport. Clarisse was further excited to see that the dress code was casual to business casual.

"It looks first class all the way," Clarisse called into the bathroom, where Roger was perfecting his beard. "It's so wonderful that we can make the trip at the same time!"

"The drug company is loaded with money. Don't get too personally flattered by the cash they tend to flash around," Roger responded. "They usually do coordinate things when they fuel up their jet."

Clarisse was suddenly puzzled. "There are two departure passes and only one return pass in the envelope." Clarisse's heart skipped a beat. "I just realized that I don't have a passport. Their instructions never mentioned anything about a passport, and the whole trip is on such short notice."

Roger quickly answered her. "I was notified late last night that I will need to stay ten days in France for business. The single return pass must be for you. The company arranges things differently for private plane passengers. It's not a problem that you lack a passport."

Clarisse would have to organize things quickly for the trip since they were to leave on the coming Saturday. She had only two days to prepare. Roger was always half-packed since he constantly traveled for work, but Clarisse had to rush her planning and packing.

Clarisse's cell phone rang. It was Marcie. "I've decided to squander a sick day from work. If you can come over today, we can coordinate what clothes we want to pack for the trip. I can whip up breakfast or brunch for us, so we get maximum girl time to plan."

As soon as Roger left for the dry cleaners, Clarisse took her suitcase and drove to Marcie's apartment. Marcie greeted Clarisse at the door, wearing old jeans and a faded t-shirt. "Here's the real me," She quipped. "What the heck. We are going to be changing and trying on clothes for hours."

Marcie motioned for Clarisse to sit down at her kitchen table. "We might as well eat now or at least decide what I can toss together. I've got a homemade potato salad I created yesterday. No need to hesitate if you like potato salad because my Mom was a caterer and overindulged in entertaining the neighbors. I learned her trade well."

Clarisse nodded yes. "I'll eat when you want to, and anything's fine." Clarisse answered.

Marcie pulled the bowl of salad and a wrapped package out of the refrigerator. "To celebrate our Buffalo heritage, I've got beef au jus from Charlie the Butcher's that I can heat up. We can use the plain Cohen's soft rolls, or I can add Charlie's weck style seasoning to the top of the soft rolls. But weck rolls do well with a beer, and we have to do without that since I don't have any beer in the house. I cook with beer, but basically, I'm a wine drinker. Your choice."

"Make things as simple as you can for yourself," Clarisse said. "It all sounds great to me. I don't have any strange diet restrictions or dislikes."

"Clarisse, I don't invite friends over. Today is a social occasion for me," Marcie said. "I've been burned big time concerning friendships. I leave all that behind at the end of the work day. But I have a good feeling about you, Clarisse. We might be in for the long haul, especially because we are family."

"Then save time, make it simple, and let me help set the table and do up the dishes after," Clarisse answered. "My mother didn't bring me up to be waited on while visiting anyone's home."

"Then let's enjoy our lunch on paper plates and zoom in on my closet," Marcie said.

Their brunchtime together was spiced with Marcie's humorous stories about her mistakes while helping her mother compete some years ago in several "Taste of Buffalo" food events.

Marcie's walk-in closet was a treasure trove of fashion. Marcie opened a bottle of wine they sipped while they laid out possible clothing combinations on Marcie's bed.

"How can one person wear all this stuff?" Clarisse asked in amazement.

Marcie shrugged her shoulders and took a sip of wine. "One person can't wear all this, which is why I seriously would like Clarisse to keep some of it. My sister was a compulsive shopper who did some modeling, and I ended up with her things in addition to mine. My Sis got tired of everything at a machinegun pace and kept giving me clothes. I just kept jamming things in my closet. It's great that we stayed the same weight. When we return from France, I swear I am sorting my clothes out. Believe me; you have no idea. There is a whole closet stuffed full in the other bedroom too. Wisely that closet is winter and fall wear while this one is spring and summer. We have to flaunt ourselves this winter with my fur jackets. Let me tell you. Those furs would pop some eyes at a hockey rink. Then there is dealing with the defeating matter: instead of furniture, the second bedroom is full of storage boxes near up to the ceiling full of heaven knows what all. If you want to help me deal out the cards, bring some good wine and a sense of humor, and we will have at it. But plan on a number of therapy sessions."

Out of curiosity, Clarisse asked, "Where does your sister live?"

Marcie hesitated. She walked over to the window and looked out. "She lived in New York City, but now it's one eight-hundred heaven with Mom and Dad."

"I'm so sorry," Clarisse said. "That's got to be awful. I'm here if you want to talk about it."

"I have to learn to deal with it, but you are absolutely correct if you think it's like falling down a bottomless pit. Let's not discuss it now. We need to prepare for our temporary escape into the intrigue of our trip to France. Believe me. You will know when I need to talk about it." Marcie took a deep breath and gave Clarisse a weak smile. "I wish I were still playing hockey to work off some of my anger, but for today let's focus on our packing."

By late that afternoon, they had packed everything of Marcie's that they both decided to take. Clarisse had a list of things she would add from her closet. Despite all the clothing choices, they concentrated on color-coordinating everything. They planned on trading off wearing one another's options to leave luggage space available for all the purchases they planned to make.

"Pretty much everything fits you. If I tone down my style and jazz up your style, we can easily pass for cousins or, at worst American tourists," Marcie said.

"Or at least two redheads that shop in the same stores," Clarisse quipped. "Your wardrobe is pretty pricey, to say the least."

"Don't forget your athletic shoes and a backpack. Pack them tonight," Marcie called after Clarisse as she left and walked over to her Toyota when ready to return home.

During both evenings before the trip, Clarisse noticed Roger seemed distracted and distant. He was back to being preoccupied with his work. The ice didn't seem as broken as she had thought it was. Right after dinner, Roger took several bottles of water and retreated to his study.

Clarisse realized that his work needed to be concentrated on to prepare for his speech at the conference. She kept her mind fixated upon anticipation concerning the trip. Clarisse waited for Roger each night, hoping he would not fall asleep in his study. She watched TV in bed for as long as she could manage to remain awake, but Roger remained isolated in the study with the door closed. She eventually double-checked the alarm each of the two consecutive nights and then fell into a much-needed sleep.

CHAPTER THIRTEEN

On the morning of their scheduled departure, Clarisse struggled to rise before the early gray of dawn. She fumbled into the bathroom, trying desperately to finish her morning routine before it inconvenienced Roger's strict and regular timing. He did not understand how long it took a woman to prepare for the day, and Clarisse wanted to look her best for the trip. The air-conditioner had stopped during the night. The apartment had become warm, and now the apartment was humid from her shower. If the air was destined to break down, it could not have selected a less-than-ideal moment. She dialed apartment maintenance and left a message that it needed to be operational before they returned in nine days.

Clarisse dressed in one of Marcie's suggested blue and beige combinations of clothing and jewelry. She pulled her hair up on top of her head and curled it just as Marcie had shown her. Clarisse noticed that when she slipped on Marcie's silk Madonna blue sleeveless tank top, her eyes no longer looked grey but reflected the blue ocean color. She smiled into the mirror and whispered, "Today, you are a poised, positive woman, ready for the adventure of a lifetime."

Clarisse was placing her luggage by the door when Roger rose and headed directly to the shower. She noticed her hiking boots in the corner of the front hall closet and thought they might come in handy due to the terrain and recent heavy rains in France. It was a long time since Clarisse had enjoyed a long walk in the woods or felt the rejuvenation a rainfall can bring. When Clarisse checked the weather in France, she saw that they had only experienced normal conditions. The rainy season was diminished, and the flowers were in bloom. She packed her boots and made several practical last-minute additions to her suitcase. She shifted a sweater and a few more incidentals in her backpack for a carry-on. She and Marcie had concluded that they had best take backpacks if they decided to walk to the nearby villages and wanted to carry small purchases back to their accommodations.

It took Roger all of his regular twenty minutes to ready himself. Clarisse had let the waves of excitement concerning the pending trip permeate through her. She was waiting by the door when Roger emerged from the bathroom. The sudden appearance of a smiling Clarisse dressed so beautifully caused Roger to catch his breath.

"You look every bit as beautiful as you did on our wedding day," Roger said as he stroked the side of her face. He paused, impulsively pulled her close, and gave her a lingering kiss.

Clarisse's heart was in her throat as she held back her tears. She hoped the day would progress in the same fashion it had begun and that the trip on the plane would give them some hours to talk together the way they had before they wed.

Roger and Clarisse no sooner negotiated the luggage out the door and onto the porch when the airport limo arrived. Clarisse had expected time to secure a cup of coffee and a bagel at the airport, only to find that they were immediately escorted down to the airport basement, where they were hurried through the metal detector archways. Their luggage only received a quick, automatic scan. The private jet was warmed up and waiting on the tarmac. Just as the sun crested the horizon, Clarisse and Roger were hurried on board as the last of the expected passengers.

Heads turned when Clarisse negotiated the aisle. Marcie and three executives were already seated. Marcie nodded and raised an eyebrow of approval concerning Clarisse's appearance. Clarisse and Roger barely had time to fasten their seat belts before the plane began to taxi. The stewardess explained the available exits and spoke the rest of her litany of flight advice. She announced that breakfast would be served as soon as they reached cruising altitude and the seat belts could be released.

Roger advised Clarisse, "I have flown this particular jet before. Be patient because breakfast is far from the ordinary fare. It's a nine-hour flight to Paris, and all the meals served will be outstanding. After that, you will enjoy an enchanting ride through the beautiful countryside on the way to Ferme de Tayac and pass a number of charming villages. Just relax and nap if you can."

Clarisse settled down with her head on Roger's shoulder. It occurred to her that either Roger had done further research concerning her motor route or else he had implied that he had visited that particular Bed and Breakfast before. She declined to disturb him to inquire. She had intended to reach for his hand, but he was already flipping through his notes and adding additional information in his native language. Even the lists that Roger made for groceries were always in French. If Roger would only leave the grocery list in the kitchen instead of in his briefcase, she could at least learn a few French words.

Clarisse closed her eyes and decided to drift off until breakfast. She made up her mind that, at home, they would have to agree on one universal language they could share. She sighed and made a mental note. It was imperative for her to achieve a command of the French language. It could only be envisioned as a permanent part of her life now. A French-English dictionary belonged on the shelf alongside her go-to cookbooks.

Marcie stayed occupied with one of the executives for the entire flight. Clarisse nodded to her, and Marcie returned her a smile. Clarisse noticed that Marcie appeared to be making fast progress with a man she did not know before the flight in progress. Marcie had mastered a technique that kept a man's attention tirelessly riveted upon her. Clarisse glanced at Roger, diligently engrossed in his speech and presentation. She decided to learn an extensive list of pointers concerning relationship management from her new friend.

Clarisse read her book or napped while Roger digested reams of information to prepare for the conference he was attending once they arrived in Paris. Clarisse hadn't been allowed any intimate time with Roger in the days before the trip. As a last resort, she had hoped for personal time with Roger during the flight, especially after the surprise morning kiss that they had shared. But her expectation quickly dwindled once he became fully absorbed in his work preparation. Clarisse made a mental note to research workaholics, their symptoms, and the daily methods of dealing with them.

Clarisse began to consider that many of the problems developing between them were due to his hanging her out to dry in favor of his employment. Perhaps he was under heavy pressure. She decided it was best to remain relatively silent, keep to her reading, and doze off as needed. At the moment, like the good wife she aspired to be, she would try to find contentment by simply sitting beside him. Although Clarisse knew that she needed to adjust to his demanding work patterns, it had gotten so extreme that it appeared to have drained the romance entirely out of him.

Clarisse had fallen asleep close to a midpoint in their flight. She awoke to the snap of the locks on Roger's briefcase. It was the first time Clarisse had a glimpse into his private work world. Realizing she was awake, he quickly shut his briefcase, but Clarisse had already seen several open boxes of medications inside. She had seen the boxes clearly enough to identify them at the local pharmacy. Clarisse decided to do that to determine what medications Roger might be taking that could facilitate his endless hours with no need for sleep.

"Are you carrying samples, or is that how you stay awake the way you do?" Clarisse murmured. She was determined to let him know he had not closed his briefcase fast enough. But she was surprised at the edgy animosity she exposed when delivering the comment.

"I must do whatever my job requires of me in the time allotted," Roger replied tersely under his breath. "Perhaps you would prefer some sort of sleep aid rather than constantly waiting up for me? If so, speak up. I have samples of all types of medications."

Clarisse said nothing as he downed the pills he already held in his hand. It would be just her luck to have married a workaholic fostering a yen to add drug addiction into the mix. She shoved the horrible thought away for reconsideration after she tracked down what drugs he was taking and looked up all the side effects.

They would have to part ways once the plane landed in Paris. He would go on his way to the seminar, and she and Marcie would be motored on about five hundred km to reach their destination. There was little conversation between her and Roger except during the meals, and even then, Roger managed only a trite conversation and maintained his distance. Now that she knew Roger was medicating himself, it occurred to Clarisse that Roger's drugs might be responsible for at least some of his changed attitude. She would have to rethink things according to the newly found piece of information. Perhaps he was trying to over-achieve out of fear of losing his job. She had recently lost hers. Clarisse made up her mind to be patient, supportive and continue to try to please her husband. They should still be in the honeymoon stage of their marriage. She would make a concerted effort to return refreshed from the trip and in a better state of mind.

It puzzled Clarisse that their meaningful time spent together hadn't only dwindled after their vows. Things had spiraled into a nose dive. Once this week was over, she made a firm resolve that she would find a way to put their relationship back on track that would bring them closer together. Even though her hope had withered on the evening she had been accepted for the trial, for a few hours, Roger had been more like the man she had chosen to marry. Clarisse held tightly to the belief that her love for Roger could pull their relationship back from whatever brink it was teetering on.

CHAPTER FOURTEEN

The executives made relatively quick exits to a waiting limo once the plane finally landed at the private airstrip.

"Have an enjoyable stay," Roger said, giving her a quick cursory kiss that held the warmth of minimal obligation. The kiss was far from the ardent passion Roger's morning kiss had held. Clarisse felt offended, but she kept it at bay, if only because it was only two hours since she had seen him take some sort of medication.

Despite Roger's attitude, Clarisse smiled briefly at him. "Is there any particular gift for you that I could shop for?" she asked him.

Roger looked eye to eye with Clarisse, which amounted to a hollow stare from his fully dilated pupils, and then he glanced away. "Clarisse, I am tight for time at the moment. The limo is waiting for me." He said, then hurried off to join the other executives.

Clarisse wanted to call after him that perhaps she should consider purchasing a few moments, but she silently bit her tongue. The depth of her frustration as it nearly rose to the surface as anger surprised her more than the look of his eyes.

Marcie immediately joined her after Roger hurried away. "So that's your handsome husband?"

"Yes. Part of the time, he claims he is," Clarisse answered as she watched Roger depart. From a distance, it appeared that Roger was familiar with the executives who had been on the plane, and he seemed in charge of the group. Roger hadn't indicated any recognition of a single one of them during the long flight. But then, he had scarcely acknowledged her while she sat beside him. All that had been accomplished on the flight was adding drugs to the already confusing equation. Knowing what he was taking might help her understand and explain what was happening to their marriage. Clarisse had a fleeting thought that perhaps their future might be a four-bedroom home, where she also had a study and took the same drugs as he did. She could sentence herself to work constantly on small business accounting and individual income tax returns.

Marcie interrupted her train of thought, "Clarisse, you look just as stunning as I knew you would."

"Thanks for the improvement clinic the other day," Clarisse joined the immediate moment and replied. "Even I can notice a dramatic change, and I like what I see."

"Well, as I said, boxes of clothes await you upon our return home. Here we are. From Buffalo to France with no one expecting even a tiny peek at my passport. I had a passport when I used to play hockey, and then I kept it up, hoping I would need it when I found the man of my dreams," Marcie remarked.

"Private jet and a private landing strip must simplify matters," Clarisse mused as she brushed aside her lingering thoughts about her relationship with Roger. "I'm just curious. How did your nine-hour investment work on the guy on the plane? He seemed spellbound."

Marcie rolled her eyes. "I let him try to hustle me every which way and lie anyway he pleased, but I wrapped it up by letting him know that I knew he was nothing but a sociopath. He needed his ego kicked. I can pick that kind of person out fairly quickly. I seldom get a nine-hour opportunity to examine the dark workings of the mind of one of those extremely tainted personalities."

"You can actually make a judgment call after nine hours or less?" Clarisse asked.

"Absolutely," Marcie answered. "That's how I cut my dating to a minimum and line out bad prospects. Once I let him think I might be a willing victim, he layers it on thicker and thicker while talking about himself until it's obvious what he is. That guy had no conscience. He bragged about how he worked his way up the corporate ladder walking over the casualties he created out of other employees who were more qualified."

"Did the guy mention what kind of work he did for Northwest? Clarisse inquired.

"He said he analyzed results and side effects on trials for new experimental drugs," Marcie answered.

"His job sounds as charming as he was," Clarisse replied. Silently she thought that could leave Roger's exact type of drug-taking a worse situation to unravel.

For a split second, a curious expression crossed Marcie's face.

"Why the look?" Clarisse asked.

"I don't know. Maybe it was an exhausting nine hours. But the thought crossed my mind that your husband looks familiar. I don't mean from the wedding photos, but maybe in just an offhand way." Marcie glanced back in the direction that the men had gone, but they had already departed. "Come on. Our limo is waiting, and I just love limo rides. We can talk while we enjoy the luxury. You'll survive a week without him. I'll make sure that we have a decent share of fun."

Clarisse pushed her thoughts away and responded to the effect of Marcie's ever-brightening smile. The road trip was enjoyable. The day was beautiful, and they were treated first-class all the way. They both relaxed in the limo and rolled the windows down to ensure a better view of Southern France. It was refreshing to see hills and valleys of greenery compared to the parched situation they both had left behind. The temperature was moderate, and the air was alive with the smell of recent rain. It revived both of them.

Marcie tapped on the driver's window. "Slow down. Take your time so we can enjoy the stunning terrain."

The driver nodded and cut back on his speed.

Marcie fluffed up her short, curly, auburn hair. "I'm surprised that they never asked if I had a perm. What an application! Talk about wanting to know every detail. Facts are facts. Clarisse, we are distant cousins. I'd even bet our hair color is pretty much the same if I discount the couple of blonde streaks that you recently added and my enhancement rinse."

"I had the streaks put in for my wedding," Clarisse answered.

"I'm impressed," Marcie commented. "Tell whoever did it that I'm their next customer. But let me ask you something. Did you really tell them everything that they wanted to know on the application, or did you keep a few secrets? I suppose they knew everything about you anyway, with your husband being one of their doctors and all."

"I'm a rather ordinary girl who's led an ordinary life. I'd have to go some to create a secret to hide," Clarisse said, locking eyes with Marcie. "My husband isn't a doctor. He's a medical advisor for the company sponsoring the clinical testing."

"Well," said Marcie while considering her response. "I never owned up to the fact that I do speak French. I believe in at least a few secrets."

"I need to learn French," Clarisse said. "Roger speaks it all the time, and I'm sure he has no time to teach me."

"No problem Clarisse. Consider it done. Lessons start when we get back home."

They silently admired the countryside as it rolled by the open limo windows.

Marcie spoke again. "I remember how I came to think that your husband was a doctor. Give or take that they say that somewhere out in the wide world, we all have a double, I recall, now that I think about it, that they addressed a man, whom I swear looked exactly like your husband, as "Doctor" at the clinic, when we did our testing. I was in the exam room when he opened the door, thinking the room was empty."

They both shrugged off the subject and returned to enjoying the view. There was no sense stoking an absurd fire, but when Marcie mentioned the clinic, Clarisse recalled thinking she heard Roger's voice several times that day. With the initial romance and the rush to marry, it had never occurred to Clarisse that to be a Medical Advisor; one would have to have a pretty hefty medical background. Roger was ten years her senior, which would give him time to have completed medical school.

Roger had never detailed anything concerning the depths of any medical studies. But when he set up his study, she had glimpsed his library shelf. It was all medical and surgical related. Somehow Clarisse had fixed it in her head that Roger was involved in reviewing cases and test studies related to various drugs. Roger hadn't ever discussed his job duties. He had always disappeared into the study before she could even attempt to squeeze things out of him, such as the name of the school he attended in Canada as a child and the town where he was born.

Clarisse decided to concentrate on her trip, and for the week, she would try to brush aside her wrestling with her marital situation. She wouldn't even consider talking to Marcie about any part of it until they returned home. Once home, she could track down Roger's medication and look at things with a fresh perspective. Her grief had tended to hang a cloud over many issues. If she found out the drugs in his briefcase were merely allergy medicine, it would shed no light on the difficulties in their marriage. But now Roger had admitted that he had samples of all kinds of drugs. What she had seen might not be all the medications that he was taking.

The conversation moved on to lighter topics. Marcie and Clarisse began to compare lists concerning the places they hoped to see and items they might shop for when they had free time away from the clinical trial. Marcie was in great spirits. Clarisse began to relax and share Marcie's enthusiastic attitude.

CHAPTER FIFTEEN

The limo pulled up near the Ferme, but it was forced to park in front of St. Marten's Church. The entrance area in front of the bed and breakfast was overloaded with various delivery trucks and several limos. While Clarisse and Marcie remained in the limo, their driver departed across the lawn and up to the bed and breakfast to acquire a luggage cart.

A stooped elderly priest, who appeared long past retirement age, paused from his task of lopping small branches off the bushes in front of the church. He silently watched as the two women emerged from the vehicle. When the breeze tugged at his cassock, it revealed the stained old work pants the priest wore underneath his church garb. His pants held stains that matched the freshly painted church door. His face seemed to pale when he caught Clarisse's eye. His expression could only be read as one of deep concern. The priest broke away from their exchanged glance and returned to the business of continuing to prune the bushes. Clarisse's immediate thought was that perhaps she could volunteer to help the priest with some tasks before her trip was over.

Clarisse and Marcie followed the driver, who had retrieved a cart, and now rolled their luggage across an acre of lawn and into the gracious entrance of the newly restored bed and breakfast. Clarisse turned back towards the church, calling a greeting to the priest, who stopped his work and waved to her in return.

When Clarisse and Marcie signed in at the desk, they were delighted to find that they had been assigned adjacent rooms. Both were given envelopes of instructions, along with their room key cards. The busy desk clerk managed a formal smile and politely welcomed them to the South of France.

"Do you know the hours of the masses at St. Marten's Church?" Clarisse asked the clerk.

The desk clerk looked surprised at the question. "I don't know if the old priest even holds services anymore. No one here associates with him," the clerk said curtly.

Clarisse visually checked the lobby for the usual rack of promotional and informational brochures concerning the local area. None were on display. Clarisse assumed some might be included within the literature commonly found in the private rooms. She was especially interested in noting any mass times at St Martin's church. It was closely located. As far as she knew, no priest ever retired from saying mass. Clarisse felt more than grateful for the opportunity to have come to France and once again have related family. If there were no services, at least she would light a few candles.

Marcie glanced at the dining area. "It must be an old home week for redheads," she laughed. "I always thought that having red hair made me an exception to the rule. But lately, I guess not."

They climbed the steep stairs to the second floor with two porters in tow, both of whom were carrying their luggage. The porters whispered to one another in French. As soon as Marcie glanced backward at them, they quickly fell silent.

"What were they saying?" Clarisse asked Marcie after the porters had left the baggage in their rooms and departed.

"Hard to say," Marcie answered with a shrug. "I'm not sure I heard what they said correctly. "I'm positive that one of them said we were very attractive, but the other said we were stupid to come here."

"Wow. I suppose that we shouldn't have given the porters a tip until they explained themselves," Clarisse said. "I guess we'll find out if we were stupid soon enough."

"Bed and breakfasts are not as formal as hotels are," Marcie mentioned. "Perhaps the casual dress code indicates that we will be expected to milk the cows before dawn and kill chickens for our dinner."

Clarisse sighed. "Maybe you misheard them. They could have meant they were stupid to work here because there is no elevator, and they have to carry luggage up steep sets of stairs."

"It's quite possible I heard it wrong," Marcie said. "Your interpretation certainly seems to fit the bill."

Clarisse had read on the Internet that the architecture of the original building had been retained throughout the resort. The private rooms were quaint, with open beams and stone walls, but the baths had been completely renovated and left nothing to be desired. The rooms were comfortably furnished with antique furniture and fresh-cut flowers gracing the side tables. From the second-story window, it was obvious that an enormous amount of money and effort had been spent to restore the buildings and grounds in such an impressive manner. It seemed an absurd investment for a place that, according to the Internet, only hosted unusually small conferences and had eleven rooms they used as guest sleeping quarters. Curiously, there appeared to be a lot of staff compared to the number of rooms used for rental revenue.

Clarisse noticed the source of the enticing aroma that encompassed the entire resort was actually emitted from the profusion of immense, old, climbing roses that graced nearly every building on the property. The rose bushes had certainly enjoyed a long life span. They had acquired substantial trunks and a network of heavy off-shooting branches, which easily enabled them to achieve their height to the second floor. Despite their apparent years of durability, heavy trellises secured each bush to the outside walls. Clarisse knew her mother would have loved admiring such impressive and substantial roses. There was no doubt that these were the same type of roses that had climbed the walls of the old English manor houses that Clarisse's mother had shown her photographs of.

While gazing out the open window, Clarisse noticed that the only awkward modern exterior addition was an in-ground swimming pool. It was situated away from the trees and centered on several acres of open lawn. Anything modern violated the old-world effect that the owners had strived to retain. The pool area fell flat to Clarisse's eye. Clarisse supposed that the public expected pool accommodations, and the pool had been treated as a more cursory budget item. Clarisse's critical judgment was that the surrounding concrete area looked like a modern afterthought. When contrasted against the old restored buildings, the finishing touch of a chain link fence surrounding the pool certainly looked out of place. But in the end, Clarisse had to admit that the aqua-blue water looked more inviting the longer she gazed at it.

Clarisse turned to Marcie. "Not to start our stay off on a bad note, but closing time rules or no, I absolutely have to slip into that pool tonight."

"I'll second that," Marcie agreed. "Let's put our swimsuits on under our clothes, and we'll see how the timing of everything works out. Coming from Western New York, what with the heat wave we have had, I'm surprised that I'm glad to notice that they have a heater unit by the pool. So even if it cools off tonight, I'm still up for a dip in the pool."

According to the directives in the envelope, they had twenty minutes left before they were expected to report to one of the downstairs private conference rooms for their induction into the clinical trial. They hurried to change and headed over to conference room number 6.

CHAPTER SIXTEEN

To their surprise, the same meticulous French woman who had been their interviewer back in Buffalo appeared to be in charge of the initial formalities of the clinical trial. "To all our participants, on behalf of our staff and funding sponsors, we all wish to say welcome to the South of France." She then briefly described the accommodations offered by the resort. There were only four other women who were also participants. Clarisse and Marcie had heard them chatting together in English before the meeting came to a semblance of order.

Marcie laughed under her breath, toyed a bit with her hair, and looked at Clarisse, who nodded that Marcie was right. They were the attractive redheads that they had seen in the restaurant earlier. An educated guess was that all the women gathered were approximately late twenties to thirty years of age.

"What's with all this expense for only six select participants?" Marcie whispered to Clarisse. "Maybe this is really a modeling contest to sell a new French drug product or cosmetic. If you happen to win, Clarisse, at least let me write your acceptance speech for you. But I warn you. I do loathe being a runner-up. When I compete, I'm nobody's…."

"Let me guess," Clarisse whispered. "You're nobody's sweet little sister. Don't worry, Marcie. With your dynamic personality, I think a shoo-in is clearly slanted in your favor."

Although the interviewer they had met when they filed their applications appeared to be in charge, she failed to introduce herself by name. Once again, the detail fanned Clarisse's annoyance. It seemed tremendously unprofessional, but Clarisse wasn't used to foreign etiquette. Clarisse didn't inquire and let the matter slide.

The woman informed the participants, "A new virus strain has emerged in Southern France. Since you all come from the United States, you each need to be inoculated immediately to preserve the clinical trial's timing. Each of you signed an agreement to the trial's terms, and although this was not specified prior, it is now necessary. You will also receive an identification badge number. For the sake of personal privacy on the trial records, you should use your badge number to identify any paper reports that need to be filled out rather than using your name. The badge number is also used in the restaurant when ordering, rather than a room identification key."

The woman appeared a bit uneasy until they all finally nodded in agreement, formed a line, and received an injection into their right shoulder. Clarisse was last in line, behind Marcie. After her injection, she turned to Clarisse, looking tight-lipped and indignant for a split second.

The woman in charge gave further instructions once all the participants were reseated. "A DNA test is needed for the trial because part of the testing involves locating and tracing specific genes related to weight loss success. Based on the findings, for the duration of the week, your meals will be provided based on the DNA testing results. The anticipated weight loss is nominal and estimated as no more than a five-pound loss over a week. Do not dispose of any unconsumed food on your dishes. The kitchen technician must deduct the leftover food from your caloric intake."

In turn, a laboratory technician began to swab the interior of the women's cheeks.

"I hope they can come up with the DNA results faster than I never got mine," Clarisse confided to Marcie.

Marcie asked the woman, "May I see my DNA analysis or have a copy?"

"No." The woman explained, "It must be kept confidential and the property of the testing consorts."

Instead of collecting a DNA sample from Clarisse, the technician advised her, "We already obtained your DNA from the International DNA Register."

Clarisse did not recall agreeing to have her DNA results released, but the technician hurried away when she tried to inquire. The technician's reaction left Clarisse with a tightened jaw. Her DNA had been placed in the International DNA Register, which apparently included sharing the results with various laboratories, even though she hadn't even received her printout of the results.

"So," Marcie whispered to Clarisse, "they are using international testing companies and data banks. Is that why they are not upfront about their names? It's pretty hard to sue nameless individuals. We've already had an unexpected inoculation, and now a weight loss program has been added based on our DNA."

Clarisse noticed Marcie didn't miss much. She suspected that beneath Marcie's easy-going exterior, a deep-seated lack of trust reigned supreme.

The unnamed woman continued her instructions. "You can expect periodic blood and urine testing. You will be restricted to the foods determined by your badge number. The kitchen will balance your diet, and you merely have to show your badge. Appropriate food will be provided to you, any time of the day or night since the kitchen is open twenty-four hours a day. Each participant's food consumption will be tracked for the benefit of the clinical trial.

"Another aspect of the testing includes using a water source that was historically owned by the old monastery, which occupied the premises many years ago. The water was sold at that time as medicinal healing water. The water well has been recently tested, and the water was determined to be ninety-nine percent pure. It will be supplied as your drinking water, and all your food will be washed and cooked in it for the duration of your stay. Some of that water has been bottled for your convenience. Please abstain from ingesting water from the showers, pool, or sink tap water since that water comes from a separate well.

"After the daily trial activities are completed, participants are encouraged to roam freely and enjoy the resort, but we do ask that you remain on the grounds. Periods of time will be arranged for touring off-premise; however, that schedule is still in the process of being drawn up. If any of you brought a passport or other valuables, please check them in with the desk clerk, and they will be locked in the Ferme's safe promptly."

"I'm in a foreign country. I am sleeping with my passport, thank you. Maybe we were stupid to think we could squeeze a little tourism out of this deal," Marcie whispered to Clarisse.

The unnamed woman directed an employee to pour herself a paper cup of water from a pitcher and drink it. All the participants were asked to do the same. They were all bid a good evening and told until morning when the DNA tests were complete, they could order what suited them from the downstairs restaurant.

Clarisse and Marcie both shared a disappointment over not being allowed to leave the premises at the end of each day. Clarisse insisted that they give it a day and then pursue an inquiry into how the arrangements for touring were progressing. She felt confident that it would be straightened out before long.

The taste of the water reminded Clarisse of the sweet, fresh spring water she had enjoyed as a child. No one had mentioned DNA-specific weight loss being part of the project, but losing five pounds wasn't a live-or-die situation in exchange for an expense-paid vacation. Clarisse made up her mind to lose her five pounds quickly. Marcie had packed an extra pair of tight jeans detailed in leather that Clarisse was dying to borrow.

Clarisse was flattered by Marcie's generosity concerning the clothing given to her. But once she realized what labels were on the clothing and the actual value of the items, she felt uncomfortable showing an interest in any particular item from Marcie's overburdened closet. Clarisse decided that once she returned and worked, she would find something special to buy for Marcie's apartment. Maybe she could help Marcie sell some of the clothing. It seemed shameful for Marcie to give away such high-cost items and get nothing in return. The donation tax write-off would never be near the value of what Marcie would contribute if she gave the excess clothes to charity. It seemed strange that her sister would wear things once and dispose of them. Clarisse's family had never been in a position to indulge in extravagant and costly clothing or, in fact, in any excesses. Family vacations had been economical but fun and few and far between. Clarisse had never longed for anything or felt she had missed out on what others had. Her life with her parents had been one of contentment that was based on values rather than efforts to have the best or the newest anything. All the money in the world could not bring her parents back. The only thing that remained now was the value system they had instilled within her and their sweet little home.

Despite their lengthy trip and long day, Clarisse and Marcie felt renewed after drinking some of the water and enjoying fresh fruit from the welcome basket in Clarisse's room. There was still an hour or more of daylight left before the evening began dropping its mantle and cloaking what was to be seen of the grounds at the Ferme.

"Here's our plan," Marcie said. "We'll explore a little and then head to supper. After that, we can slip into the pool. Or if we aren't that hungry, we can hit the pool before supper. I recommend we put towels in our backpacks and take them with us."

"Flexibility sounds good," Clarisse answered while she jammed two bath towels into her backpack. Just in case, we better take along some underwear. We might need to get out of our wet swimsuits if supper follows our swim. Grab your backpack. We can use it to carry dry clothes."

CHAPTER SEVENTEEN

Clarisse and Marcie took several bottles of spring water and headed outside to explore the grounds. They were in no rush for dinner when they had access to a restaurant with no cutoff time specified when food would stop being served. They walked the grounds and admired the old architecture. They followed the resort map paths to various buildings and locations. The early evening air was cool enough to be refreshing, especially when coupled with the gentle breeze. Everything the eye could see was part of an idyllic and stunning setting. Even the stone utility building, called "the old cheese house," was enhanced by a tumble of old roses that reached the roof and created a shaded canopy below. Everything about the place seemed to whisper to Clarisse that she should set her troubles aside, inhale deeply and indulge herself in her relaxing surroundings.

They located the equestrian barn and extensive trails mapped out in their resort booklet. Clarisse began to head for the table by the cascading roses, but Marcie took her arm and led her directly into the stables. They appeared to be alone in the barn. A French notation on the blackboard, which Marcie translated, explained that it was the usual supper hour for the barn employees.

Eighteen horses were sequestered in roomy stalls that lined each side of the charming old-world style stable. Marcie stopped to speak softly to each horse in turn. She called them by the names etched in brass on the individual stall doors. She encouraged Clarisse to stroke the sides of their faces once the horses became curious and projected their heads over the heavy wooden stall doors.

The tack room and a grooming area were located off the center aisle at the midway mark. Marcie pointed out that the individual saddles and bridles were on the racks and identified with each specific horse's name. She explained to Clarisse that a saddle and bridle must fit perfectly. It surprised Marcie that all the horses had such expensive and spotless tack.

Marcie mentioned, "It's odd an eleven-room Bed and Breakfast can afford to support the expense of such quality horses and tack unless someone was leasing the right to use them in exchange for perhaps using the stable."

"You ride, don't you?" Clarisse asked, after seeing Marcie knew her way around a stable exceptionally well.

"Yes, and I can teach you if you like. It's something extra we can do while we are detained on the grounds," Marcie answered. "Now, here is the best horse for you." Marcie made her way back down the central aisle, over to the stall of a dapple grey mare. She opened the stall door and hooked a lead line onto the mare's halter. The horse ambled out of the stall and onto the dirt-floored aisle. Marcie led the horse to the grooming area and tied her off in the aisle. She beckoned Clarisse until she stood in front of the mare. "See how she bows her head in front of you?" Marcie asked. "It means she accepts your presence. She has indications of gentle temperament and the correct conformation, which means less of a bumping in the saddle for a brand new rider."

Clarisse could see the horse was responding to her touch. It began to give her a soft nudge or two. She reached up and stroked the horse's thick black mane. "Then let's plan on my being your student, but promise me that you won't allow me to be a quitter," Clarisse said. She was in a different environment and suddenly decided to do something bold for a change.

"The mare expects that we will take her out for exercise since I took her out of her stall, so we have to treat her to something. Lesson one is brushing her off. Marcie left, returned with the horse's grooming box, and proceeded to show Clarisse the routine grooming procedure before riding. Clarisse watched as Marcie deftly used a hoof pick on the underside of the horse's hoof. "See the center part?" Marcie asked.

Clarisse nodded.

"In America, we call it the f-r-o-g," Marcie whispered and then smiled. "Not a word you should toss around in front of a Canadian Frenchman back home."

Clarisse laughingly agreed.

One of the employees suddenly appeared at the entrance to the barn. She called a greeting to them and approached. "Riding is included with your stay at your option," she told them warmly. "Just add your names to the blackboard and note what horse you wish to use on what day, and it will be saddled and ready for you here at the end of the day's normal activities. Jumps are set up in one of the arenas in back of the barn. You are most welcome to use them if you like. The trails are quite picturesque and enjoyable. If you use the blackboard, you do not need to know how to speak any French. If you find that you have any questions during your stay, you may ask for me. My name is Marie," she said as she patted the rump of the grey mare. "If you are new to riding, this is the best horse for you." She departed as quickly as she had arrived.

"Now I'm sure we won't go stir crazy while they figure out when we get to tour a little. We can ride on the trails and at least view the countryside from afar," Marcie said after they finished the grooming and led the mare back to her stall.

Despite the fact that they appeared to be alone, Marcie motioned to Clarisse to step outside of the barn. She whispered low to Clarisse, "When we got inoculated, they were watching me while they spoke in French. It's in none of my school records, but I learned French from my Grandmother. Don't ever let on that I can understand what they are saying!"

"I won't," puzzled Clarisse, "not even under extreme torture." She responded while looking quizzically at Marcie.

Marcie's blue eyes were beginning to seethe, but she continued in a low whisper, "You were the last one to get the injection. Right? After I was given my identification badge, the man standing behind the desk answered his cell phone. He said, "All the fatted calves have been microchipped." Feel where they injected me! Press in hard. Do you feel it?"

Clarisse could feel a solid bump and then felt the same hardness in her own arm. They headed over to the open area by the pool.

"As soon as I am back in the states, I will definitely have it removed," Marcie ranted. "If we walked off these grounds, they could find us. There's no reason to subject us to a thing like this unless they plan on tracking us, perhaps forever. Why and what for? They certainly were not upfront about what they did. With all the talk of this government and that one wants to microchip everyone, they could have injected us with a chip they need to test."

Clarisse had no answer, but she decided to have an incision made as soon as she returned to the States. "Marcie, if that is what they did, it's outrageous. I've heard of microchipping pets, but microchipping individuals without their permission would be crossing too close to the line, which I call freedom. We are best off remaining calm and closely watching what's going on. But in order to find anything out, it's best to keep quiet and play along for at least right now."

"Don't tell your husband," Marcie added. "I can't help it. I still think he was at the clinic, whether you believe it or not, and if that's true, things are somehow genuinely screwed up. For starters, let's try to figure out what's going on."

"Pull yourself together, Marcie. Maybe we are just overthinking things. I won't tell anyone, not even Roger," Clarisse said, taking Marcie firmly by the shoulders. "Privately, we can exchange our thoughts every day when we go riding."

"If we're livestock, then no better place to hang out but by the barn." Marcie gave a half-desperate shrug and reset her composure. "For now, let's go get fatted. You never know. It might be our last decent meal for a week."

The evening had begun to cast a failing light. Only one of the underwater pool lights was on as they began to walk by the pool. The air started to cool, and steam was curling as it rose from the water. Clarisse spotted a staff member skimming the water and checking the chemicals. "Is the pool closed already?" Clarisse asked him.

"Ten usually," He answered using perfect English. "But the staff is allotted time in the pool from ten until midnight, so you are free to join them later if you like. They're all lifeguards, so management does not care. You can swim now if you like. I just tested the water, and it's perfect chemically. Not only that, but it looks like the timer on the pool heater isn't working as it should. The pool water usually maintains at seventy-five, and it's currently at ninety-five degrees. You two couldn't pick a better night or time to go in."

"Let's go in now for a short time," Marcie said. "I expect wine with dinner, and it's been a long day. I don't think I'm up to hanging out with the staff tonight, besides he had to turn the heater off, and the water temperature will keep dropping."

"Maybe later," Clarisse said.

"Perhaps I will see you later then," he answered. "I have to see if we have another pool light on hand and locate where the lifeguard on duty got to. He's off taking an extra break somewhere because he thought I'd be by the pool longer than I needed to be."

After he walked away, Clarisse and Marcie went to the dark side of the pool and began stripping down to their swimsuits.

The water was relaxing and a delicious contrast to the cooling night air. It was unusual for two individuals to have a huge Olympic size pool all to themselves. They made the most of it, but they kept their swim quiet to make their privacy last. After a short duration of time, Clarisse and Marcie stood together in the water on the dark side of the pool. The night air was rich with the fresh scent of the thriving greenery. The steam lent a dreamy effect to the gloriously warm water. Suddenly, footsteps began approaching along the concrete sidewalk. Two men were speaking French quietly as they slowly walked past the pool area.

Marcie motioned for Clarisse to keep quiet.

After the men had passed by and were sufficiently clear of the surrounding area, Marcie spoke in a whisper. "I know what I heard. He said, 'Let's keep it clean of Village rumors. This batch is best not let off of the premises. Then the other man asked how they could keep the old priest in line. The first guy said that the old priest gets to live there until he dies, which hopefully could happen any day. Then the church finally gets demolished. The old priest knows nothing. He's upset because we have possession of the medicinal well he has used for years. He won't come here. What can one old priest do? What is he going to do? Fight us all with just a bottle of holy water? A couple of these calves are high-ranking stuff, so we need to keep things operating smoothly. Our job is to run a host establishment, and that means no meddling in the property owner's affairs. It makes no difference if the clinic trial ends a day early. They've already paid our full annual contract fee, which is big bucks to us. Then he told the second man to send the whole staff home early, around 6 PM Thursday but to wait until nearly six to tell them."

Clarisse and Marcie slipped out of the pool when it seemed positive that the coast was clear. They quickly towel-dried and ran to the bathhouse to change into their dry clothes. They casually walked back towards the main building.

"Don't even think of calling your husband. The company he works for sent us here. We need to find out more if we can. We have until Thursday to get with the priest and see what he knows," Marcie whispered as they walked across the grounds.

"Marcie, I agree. We need to know more. It makes no sense. This is the second time someone referred to us as beef on the hoof. It sounds like some sort of slavery market going on. They may be watching, so for tonight over dinner, let's just talk about ourselves. That will seem totally natural. But I think we should consider sneaking around in order to stay in the same room at night."

Marcie agreed. "We might have to run away to the Village, but we have to do it at the right moment, and I only have a few days to teach you to ride in a passable fashion."

"All I know about Marcie is that she has one quick temper, knows a lot about horses, enhances her hair color, misses little, and is highly suspicious. I honestly would have copied some of the family information, but we got here so fast that there wasn't much time except to plan what to pack. We will get into the family information at some point. I promise."

"Can't you slip me a tiny crumb or two of the family history?" Marcie begged her in an exaggerated tone of voice.

"No. Not until I learn how to at least get on and off a horse gracefully," was Clarisse's firm reply. "You may find me a pretty challenging riding student, and I need to be sure you don't give up on me."

"I'll have you riding well by Thursday," Marcie said. "I even have the perfect graduation present in mind for you, provided you're not a quitter."

"I'm relaxing too much now. We better think about heading to dinner," Clarisse replied.

CHAPTER EIGHTEEN

By the time they were seated and placed their order, the other women were already leaving the restaurant. Clarisse and Marcie enjoyed their meal in a fair amount of privacy and even split a bottle of wine on the terrace. Their food likes and dislikes were remarkably similar. Marcie disliked when advertisers expressed little regard for their consumers. Clarisse hated the way the larger clients showed disregard for their employees.

Marcie disclosed that she had lost her sister and parents in an auto accident a little over a year ago. Clarisse had lost her parents in precisely the same way and within the same time frame. They both admitted that having no family left made fostering a lasting relationship with a newly found shirt-tail cousin rather appealing. Clarisse admitted how deeply the loss of her parents affected her and how much better it felt to express it to someone who had a similar experience.

Marcie was bold and animated, which fit perfectly with her career in advertising. She was hotter-headed than Clarisse, who was extremely timid, even for an accountant. But all in all, they deepened their friendship, and by the time the bottle of wine was nose down on the ice, it was apparent to both of them that they shared the same humor and, more importantly, the same personal values. The one difference seemed to be that Clarisse had a more religious upbringing, which had remained solidly with her. Marcie had a long list of family-cultivated doubts about organized religion.

Marcie proposed a toast with their final glass of wine, "Here is to the South of France, and may we share our friendship and shore one another up, no matter what our future lives hold in store."

Every morning, they took an early breakfast on the terrace. Their allowed foods were identical, and to their relief, their diets did not seem highly restricted. The following days were filled with weight loss plans and exercise levels to complement the specific diet that suited their individual DNA results. Cardiac testing was completed, as well as confidential counseling sessions concerning cholesterol readings.

Clarisse received short messages from Roger, always left with the desk clerk. She left him telephone messages back but received no direct calls from him. Clarisse had become beyond irritated with his conduct. She guessed it would have been a rather complicated journey home, sitting next to him without discussing it.

Lunch became a midday highlight during their stay, but they changed their clothes and headed straight to the barn when the clinical day was over.

Now that they were riding every day, Clarisse was grateful that, at the last minute, she had decided to pack her hiking clothes. Marcie was surprised at how easily Clarisse took to riding. Just as Marcie had predicted, the grey proved an excellent horse to help hone Clarisse's new skill. Marcie leased a horse at a barn back in the states, and she was sure a couple of friends of hers could lend Clarisse a horse so they could continue riding together. They both enjoyed exploring the extensive property. They searched several small caves in the hope that there might be some trace of a prehistoric cave painting.

They had been at the Ferme for five days but still had not been allotted time to do any touring off of the premise. Marcie continually asked about it, but she was put off by being told the trial was behind schedule and that they would try to fit something in. Both of them were quietly scrutinizing everything that transpired. Clarisse laughed at most of Marcie's observations. She suggested that Marcie should consider a career change and become a professional investigator.

CHAPTER NINETEEN

On the sixth day of breakfast on the terrace, Marcie saw the old half-hunched priest trudging down the road towards St Martin's. She called to him and waved. To her surprise, the old priest slowly came across the lawn and then towards their table.

Marcie whispered to Clarisse as the old priest approached the table. "It seems we are destined to be sent home, having seen nothing but this place. At least, maybe we can take a look at his church."

"You're right, and I should go to mass," Clarisse mentioned.

"Greetings, Father," Marcie said. My name is Marcie Michel-Laurent, and this is my newfound cousin Clarisse Michel-Laurent."

Father Dubois appeared a bit winded, nervous, and shaken. Clarisse assumed it was from his exhausting walk, which had been slightly uphill across the lawn. They immediately invited him to catch his breath and sit down at the table with them.

Clarisse offered the priest her glass of water. After several sips and moments, he seemed to recover and steady himself.

"I am Father Dubois. I used to take many a meal here," he said, tapping his sagging paunch. "From America, are you?" he said, scrutinizing them both over the top of his wire-rimmed eyeglasses, but in the end, he seemed to be focusing hard on Clarisse. "I know of your family name from records at the church; however, none with that name remain around here. I hate to date myself, but I am close to ninety years old now, and St. Martins has claimed all but a few of those years."

Clarisse noticed a keen glint of intelligence rooted deep in the priest's eyes. He almost appeared to be considering how much he should disclose to them. It was a lucky source for them to happen upon the priest. He had lived in the area for nearly ninety years.

Marcie inquired if St. Martin's Church was considered on the resort's grounds. He acknowledged that the inn owned and used the grounds, but the church building was now leased back to the Catholic Church. The Priest said the transaction had been accomplished during the last few months. He further informed them that the church had long been a historically protected building that required constant maintenance. He made his best effort to take care of the building.

When Marcie asked who had purchased the resort, the priest looked down quickly and said in a whisper, "I am an old man, unsure of many things, but I have seen much in my days." He tore a piece of paper from Clarisse's notepad and pulled a pencil out of his cassock. "You are Catholics?" he inquired.

They both nodded.

"Here are the times of the masses," he said. "Few people know that St Martin's faces the Northwest," he paused. "Shall I expect you around 6 PM this evening? I will be pleased to give you both a tour of the church."

"Why thank you so much, Father," Clarisse replied. "That is what we were hoping for."

The interviewer spotted Father at their table and then hurried across the restaurant floor. "I thought you no longer came here, Father Dubois," she said tersely.

"As a rule, I no longer do," he said. "These lovely ladies called me over to inquire about the times my masses are said. Some Americans, it seems, still attend such functions." He made it a point to give Marcie and Clarisse a lengthy blessing. "He defiantly looked the interviewer in the eye and said, "Last I checked, my blessings last a good while, long past when you wipe off the table." The priest immediately rose from his chair and departed.

Annoyance was clearly written on the interviewer's face as the old priest departed. "Foolish old man," She muttered in French as she walked away.

"The church faces due east," Marcie curiously commented.

"Maybe he was implying Northwest Pharmaceuticals," Clarisse whispered. "They must own this place now. It makes sense. We are here, aren't we? And we came on their plane?"

"Clarisse, now you're the one who shows promise as an investigator," Marcie replied. "It does add up when you consider how confidential he acted when he made the remark. It was odd how rude that woman was to him. Now figure that one out."

"Oh, that one is easy," Clarisse answered. "He meant she could use a little saving grace, and she was not having any of it."

CHAPTER TWENTY

Before the day's required clinic attendance began, Marcie and Clarisse asked that a few packed sandwiches be prepared. They picked up their bag meal at five. They then headed back to their rooms to change before visiting with the priest. Still hoping to ride that evening, they dressed accordingly.

Roger had left a message at the desk explaining that he was exhausted. He still had to attend a dinner that evening. He said he would call whenever he was available, but it would likely be tomorrow. Clarisse hadn't spoken to him in six days. She was so angry with him that she could have cared less. She made up her mind to come clean about her situation to Marcie once they returned home. It would be a positive step to see what Marcie's thoughts were about the way Roger was acting.

After Clarisse had changed her clothes, there was a soft knock on the door. The maid bringing extra towels for her room happened to be the woman named Marie, whom Marcie and Clarisse had met at the barn.

After placing the extra linens, she addressed Clarisse, "You have done very well learning to ride."

"I have to say I have enjoyed your barn immensely. In fact, I will continue to ride when I return to the states."

Marie lowered her voice to a scarcely heard whisper. "Father Dubois is an old man, but he is a good man and a friend to many in the village." Clarisse noticed a significant edge in her tone and a fire of determination in her eyes. Marie resumed a normal tone of voice. "I am always most pleased to meet Americans," Marie said as she reached for Clarisse's hand and shook it.

Clarisse felt the folded paper Marie had slipped into the palm of her hand. She held eye contact with Marie and responded, "Please wait, and thank you for making my stay such a pleasant one." Clarisse slid the note into her purse, then drew out a tip and gave it to Marie, who thanked her profusely.

As Marie left, she suddenly turned back to Clarisse before shutting the door. With an expression of genuine concern on her face, she said, "My prayers are for your safe journey back to America."

Despite discounting Marcie's fear that there were more eyes and ears in the rooms than could be seen, Clarisse had gone along, with only discussing things with Marcie during their daily jaunts on horseback. Marcie was even careful when in proximity to the horses, suggesting that the saddles might carry listening devices. Although Marcie was acting neurotic at times, Clarisse still enjoyed Marcie's company far too much; to let Marcie's suspicions over little things override their developing friendship. The way the maid conducted herself led Clarisse to suspect that Marcie might be on the right track. She did not open the note immediately; instead, she put it off until privacy during the walk to the church would provide an ideal opportunity to read the message.

The next knock on her door was Marcie's. "I guess tonight will be our final ride together at the Ferme, so I brought you your graduation present. Not that we won't get together and ride some back home, but this is still a momentous occasion." Marcie pulled the leather-trimmed jeans out of her backpack. "They are all yours. They will look better on you than they do on me anyways." Marcie stuffed the jeans into Clarisse's backpack.

Clarisse was stunned for a moment. She thanked Marcie profusely and offered to lend the jeans back to her whenever she desired.

"Consider it step one to improving your wardrobe or my way of bonding. You look really good with splashes of color added. Whatever I lent you to wear for the trip is yours to keep. Don't say no. I know where to come if I need to borrow it back. For tonight we better take a change of clothes along in our backpacks," Marcie said. It's looking like rain. We could get stuck out by the cave for a while, and we'll feel better if at least our clothes are dry."

Storm clouds had begun to gather in the distance. "What do you make of this?" Clarisse asked Marcie as they made their way across the lawn on the way to the church. She passed the priest's note to Marcie. "Marie was so secretive when she delivered this that I was unsure what the note might contain."

The note, left with Clarisse, was written in the priest's elderly handwriting, "Come to the back door of the church." Beneath that, there was a scratched notation. It appeared to read, "B negative to the power of one."

"Well," Marcie said after looking at the note, "I guess we now know that he won't be at the front door. But oddly enough, I heard someone say that phrase in French in the hall. You know, the B negative expression? It makes no sense to me. Maybe", she widened her eyes and laughed, "It's a secret password. I know you think I'm half out of my mind with all my suspicions. You have to admit that there have been unusual details that have emerged during our vacation/slash clinical trial participation. Perhaps Father can help shed some light on a few things. Let me question him. I can be relentless until I get the answers I need."

"Don't be unmerciful with questions," Clarisse said. "He did mention he was almost ninety years old."

"Then he ought to know quite a bit about our ancestors and whatever is really going on at the Ferme," Marcie countered.

CHAPTER TWENTY-ONE

They knocked on the rear door of the church. The wind picked up sharply while they patiently waited until they heard the click of at least six locks. The old priest beckoned them to hurry and enter. Once inside the church, Marcie helped him push the door closed against the whipping wind. He relocked and bolted the church door.

"A lot of locks just to keep the wind out," Marcie whispered to Clarisse under her breath.

Marcie began to query the priest almost as soon as he locked the door. "Father, we came to ask what you know of our family's history. Clarisse's relative lived at the monastery, and I am related to one of the Michel-Laurents, who was one of his brothers by birth.

"Ah, yes. Political times were exceedingly difficult. One day people were Catholics, and the next, they were not, depending on who was currently in charge of the local area. It was a large family, and one of the brothers would not play the game. He took to the monastery for any protection that could be offered. He was never a religious brother, so to speak, but rather a mason by trade and an accomplished artist too. He did much for St Maximum's and St Martin's. He married and had his children when he was up in years. A good family, so it was said. In fact, historically, part of your family helped locate and excavate the sacred healing source of water at the Ferme." The old priest beckoned them into a small, dusty room used as his study.

The priest continued, "Actually, the whole family was baptized here. I looked it up. The church, this church, any church or monastery, used to offer refuge for those oppressed. This church has almost been my entire life and only parish. Now they have taken the sacred ground from beneath it and seek to sweep established religion away. There is so much history gathered here that is soon to come to an end. Please, both of you, will you share some tea with me?"

They both agreed and settled down in the dust-coated armchairs across from his rickety desk.

"Many changes have taken place over the years," the priest said while watching their faces closely. "Times have changed but not necessarily for the best; out with the Latin, in with the new. I still cling to the Latin Mass. Those that come are grateful for that connection to the past." He hesitated and then continued, while focusing on Clarisse, "I did not think I would live to see evil come knocking at Christ's door. They leave me here to console and quiet the local folk while they reap their harvest. They know I have almost lost the strength to help anyone, even if it's only to the path of their redemption. Now they even own our sacred well, and I can no longer offer my traditional healing mass."

The old priest's hand shook as he poured the tea from a large teapot. He took a flask off the table, added a few drops into each cup, and blessed the tea. He half smiled and shook his head. "Holy Water is my only protection. I have come to drink a bit of it in my tea. My Marie brings me a bit of water from the well, which seems to continue to sustain me. The monastery used to ship it all over the world to use for healing masses. It was considered a powerful source of healing in times of great need."

Clarisse reached into her purse and gave Father Dubois a bottle of water from the well.

"Thank you, my child," he said. "Perhaps your generosity has added a few days onto the life of a terribly old man. Now, are you both here because you are mere travelers from America? Since the property purchase, there has been some activity over there. But you two are the first to be guests there and also come to visit my church."

"We were brought here for a week for a clinical trial," Clarisse answered. "But while we were here and had the opportunity, we wanted to find out as much as possible about the area and past generations of our family."

"Of course, you are being paid a good sum for participating in the clinical trial, or what have you?" he asked.

They nodded.

"My Marie keeps me aware of many disheartening things that transpire at the Ferme." He paused and sipped his tea.

"I do know that many years ago, the families fled the area, or they were taken," the priest said.

"What do you mean by taken?" Marcie asked as her eyes widened.

"The women disappeared. At first, they were either enticed with money or simply taken in the night by strangers. But when even the youngest of them began vanishing, the families moved out of the area and scattered. You both are proof that some of them had the good fortune to make the voyage to America."

Marcie unpacked the sandwiches that she had brought. The three of them silently ate and sipped their tea. The sound of the pendulum on the study wall clock filled the room. Now and again, they could hear the wind batter at the bolted church door.

The old priest finally broke the silence. "So you see, while I have old baptismal records, I do not know exactly where your families scattered. Soon perhaps, I will not have those records, so I pulled them out for you to keep. He took several heavy thick envelopes off of his desk and handed them to Marcie. Here are the baptismal certificates for the entire family. They are all originals since I have no way to copy anything. Perhaps they will be useful as part of your family's history."

Marcie and Clarisse thanked him profusely.

Marcie opened one of the envelopes. "Some of the birth certificates date back over one hundred years ago. These are priceless to us Father!" She exclaimed as she placed them in her backpack.

The priest's gaze fell upon Clarisse. He studied her closely. "You are possibly aware of an evil force that lies hidden? The veins that carry its lifeblood have spread through many countries, and now it even owns the ground I walk on. Their powers are far-reaching." He paused and looked over his glasses in a questioning manner at them both. "It is dangerous for you to be at Ferme de Tayac. It is so close to the heart of the matter." The clock chimed while the priest waited for a response but to no avail.

The tea seemed to have a positive yet mystical effect on all three of them. Time seemed to suspend itself as if waiting for clarity to catch up to it. Visually, the priest seemed a bit more vibrant as he poured himself a second cup and refilled theirs.

They drank tea in deafening silence, except for the sound of Father Dubois' spoon dragging against the inside of his teacup while he continually stirred his tea. It was a few long moments until Clarisse inquired further.

"Father, precisely what is the heart of the matter?" Clarisse ventured, still baffled by his words.

"I guess I was in error assuming that you knew more of the history of this area. The blood, I should say, the B negative bloodline, flowed heavily throughout this section of France," the priest answered. He seemed a bit frustrated that his message was not coming across. He sighed heavily and made another attempt to explain. "The holy church denies the bloodline of Christ and has not protected it. Now it is to be used for evil purposes, to sustain a New World Order, and bring into being the reign of the dark one. It is abundantly clear; they need a ready supply of B-negative blood and organs for transplants, not to mention breeding stock, as a final insult to Christ."

Clarisse and Marcie looked at the priest in silent disbelief and then at one another.

"Surely what I say is not so outrageous if you have heard of a New World Order?" said Father Dubois, with more than a hint of exasperation. "They need to ensure a ready blood supply as they attempt their project; to defy the finality of death and produce the Anti-Christ. My Marie works next door now. She says the "fatted calves," as that New World Order calls them, are all being made to wear the mark of the beast. With that mark upon you, they can find you anywhere, but it is highly unlikely they will allow you to return to America. Marie says that you were brought to France on a private jet, and you will all disappear, just like the rest. Lambs to the slaughter, she calls it." The priest intensely studied their reactions.

Marcie's hand automatically found her shoulder, and Clarisse followed her thinking.

The priest motioned for them to follow him. He walked to the inside of the front door of the church and dropped a beam across it to lock it for the night. He motioned them over to the Holy Water fountain at the front of the church. Clarisse automatically blessed herself, as was the custom. The priest glanced at Marcie and waited. She dipped her fingers in the water and made the sign of the cross.

"As you know, it is a common practice to bless yourself when entering a Catholic Church. But the water's purpose, at the church's entry, has long been forgotten. It was placed there to show other members of the congregation that they were safe because you entered with your soul in good standing. Once a soul wholly belongs to the evil one, Holy Water plays tremendous havoc on the physical body. An evil soul cannot enter a body that contains Holy Water. Baptism is symbolic of that belief. Few people actually drink Holy Water, but it is recommended, for some, in times of emergency." The priest walked over to the Baptismal Font. He poured the bottle, of the healing source water, into the baptismal font, blessed the water, and then filled his flask. "Take this flask and share it," He said to Clarisse. "I have other flasks I can use."

After a brief struggle and great effort, the priest slid the Baptismal Font to the side. "I placed the font here as a deterrent to the unwanted souls." He unscrewed an old olive wood panel from where the carved wainscoting had joined. "This is the entrance to the old stone grotto upon which this church was built. Few have ever seen it, and it is long forgotten. The staircase and grotto were built by your ancestors."

They descended a steep, winding, narrow stone staircase. The temperature continued dropping as they progressed. The smell of must became thick and heavy in the air.

CHAPTER TWENTY-TWO

The priest shuffled in the darkness. When he lit several oil lamps, an exquisite painting of a red-haired Madonna and child revealed itself in the flickering light. The detailed, emotionally touching depiction caused Clarisse to catch her breath. She reached over and reverently touched the frame.

"The painting called the Magdalene and Child was painted by your relation," the priest said to Clarisse. "I hid it here before they inspected the property for the purchase. It was originally kept behind the altar in the church."

"Father Dubois, what will become of the painting?" Clarisse asked. "It cannot be left to deteriorate in this damp grotto."

"My Marie will place it in safekeeping as soon as possible. Only a few can be trusted during these turbulent times," answered the priest.

From behind the beautiful painting, he produced an old, dusty roll of parchment. On the outside, written in faded, flourished script, was the word "Clarisse." The priest's hands began to tremble, and his eyes filled with tears. "This has been handed down many generations to be given to someone named Clarisse. When you told me your name, I knew you had finally come here to receive it." He placed the parchment in her hands. "It is a copy of the bloodline of Christ, which was secretly kept at St. Maximum church. It continues on for many generations. I have added names from my baptismal record files concerning those born, who were born here, but it is far from complete. The bloodline has traveled to many other countries. I can only assume that maybe you are to explore it further, to protect others." He pressed her hands around the old parchment.

Clarisse and Marcie were stunned at the revelation.

Again the priest fumbled but this time into a niche in the stone wall. He withdrew a thin leather bag. "I have only one weapon left, which even the Holy Father does not know of," the priest said. "It came from St. Maximum's church and was handed down to me." He opened the leather bag. It held a short silver knife with a crucifix fashioned into the handle. "It is told that inside the handle is hidden a lock of the hair of Christ's daughter Sarah, and a lock of hair from the Magdalene, as well as one from the sacred head of Christ, himself. This knife, too, belongs to you now. It is said that it can terminate not only the body but the soul of a demon."

"It holds the DNA of Christ!" Marcie murmured as the silver knife shimmered in the flickering flames of the oil lamps.

Clarisse felt her knees weaken.

"I entrust to you the most valuable Christian relic in the world," the priest said. "I am certain that the New World

Order knows nothing of this relic. They are busy searching and mapping the DNA of those with B-negative blood. In my ninety years, I have never heard that they know to quest after a silver knife from the South of France that could end the life of any demon, including the Anti-Christ. You must never reveal its contents until neither of you can keep it safe any longer. It must never be defiled. Keep its secret within your bloodline. We cannot afford an enemy within the ranks. We all must pass this test." He dipped the tip of the knife into the flask of Holy Water and touched his palm lightly. Nothing transpired.

"No mark is, in fact, the mark of a good soul," he said.

He handed the knife to Marcie, who touched her palm with no result. She then took Clarisse's shaking hand and touched her palm with the knife, and there was no reaction.

"Seeing is often necessary to believe when the mark of the beast is concealed," the priest said and looked at Marcie. He reached over and dipped the knife into the Holy Water. He lightly touched the blade's tip to the site of Marcie's injection. The smell of seared flesh filled the grotto.

Confusing thoughts filled Clarisse's mind. Marcie was sure they had microchipped her arm, and she insisted that things were amiss at the clinic. Clarisse supposed that the strange burning reaction had occurred because of Marcie's staunch beliefs. Marcie reached over and quickly touched the knife to Clarisse's injection site. The burning sensation made Clarisse scream out in pain.

"They cannot track you now by the mark they gave you, but I know they are familiar with the local area and have eyes everywhere. Trust only what my Marie tells you both to do."

The priest sadly shook his head. "Even an old priest can be found to be a sinner. I wept for proof of forgiveness for years because in a moment of weakness, although it is not known to others beyond Marie and now both of you, it was I who fathered Marie. Now I have come to understand the purpose of her birth. The Lord has His purposes and works in many strange ways that we should not question."

The priest wrapped the knife back into the leather bag and slipped it into the leg pocket of Clarisse's cargo pants. "I am so old that perhaps my hours are numbered, for it appears my final purpose is now complete. Marie has told me that tonight, they would take the women deep into the wine cellar, and after plying them with wine, they will be kept there in isolation. The women will then be herded off to their respective fates."

The lamplight enhanced the appearance of age upon the priest, but his fervor burned within him brighter than the flames. "You must be Clarisse's protector. She does not yet see the strength within her," the priest said to Marcie. "Believe that all things are possible and be strong."

Marcie set her jaw, firmly determined to protect her friend.

"You, my gentle child," the priest said, holding Clarisse by the shoulders. "You must reach inside and gather your strength for what lies ahead. Tonight we can only try to free a pitiful few. You both must evade capture. You both carry with you information that is critical to so many."

Clarisse had always found that her strength from within habitually fell short. Tonight the fear of her shortcoming felt overwhelming to the point of being painful.

The priest continued, "You both must fully understand that you are fighting for your lives. They believe they own you and that your every bone, organ, and pint of blood is theirs for the taking. They believe the decisions of if and when you take your next breath are theirs to make. You are expendable to them if need be, for there are many others in the bloodline."

Clarisse staggered under the weight of his words.

"Look at your arm," Father said to Clarisse. The burn had already healed into the shape of a cross. "Take strength in the cross, my child," he said firmly. "You are destined to help preserve the lineage of Christ from a terrible fate. It was determined long before you were born. Come, we must hurry now. My Marie is waiting with her brothers. Trust them. They will help you both escape the evil fates that were planned for you."

The priest took one of the old oil lamps down from the wall and beckoned them to follow. "This tunnel takes you back to the Ferme. It emerges by the old cheese storage house near the stable.

CHAPTER TWENTY-THREE

The gravel crunched beneath their steps as they followed the slow pace of the priest along the passageway until they could see the light up ahead. Marie's brothers had rolled the entrance stone back in order to open up an exit from the tunnel.

Father Dubois took Marie's hand in his. "Marie, my child, stay safe tonight and always. They have what we have been waiting to gift them," the priest said. "May God be with each and every one of you." The priest said a brief blessing over Marie and her brothers. Once he retreated inside the tunnel, the stone concealing the entrance was replaced.

Marie took the two women aside. "The calves are all corralled in the wine cellar. They do not even know they are locked in. They have been left with two armed guards while the rest are searching for the two of you. They think you are still on the grounds because your microchips did not set off an alarm." Marie glanced quickly at the crosses on the shoulders of Clarisse and Marcie. "There is no time to take you away at the moment. We need to try to save the other four, too. As soon as they went to search the grounds, I removed the women's files from the clinic office. The files document the fate of all the women who have been funneled through the Ferme.

"All of my brothers are well-armed. They have cut the sleeves off of their shirts. That is how you will know not to shoot at them. Word was sent out that all regular employees were dismissed for the night. My brothers will gain access to the kitchen wine cellar entrance to free the captives and bring them out to safety. The alarm will go off when they enter the main building, probably bringing the consort members out in the open. But it may also bring the local police within little more than half an hour. As of now, there are six against us who are loose on the grounds, two in the building, and the plane is expected to arrive with several more.

"When we need to leave, there are horses tethered in the largest of the caves, facing the Northwest side of the barn. Take these, and do not be afraid to use them," Marie said as she shoved handguns and shells into the hands of Clarisse and Marcie. "Try to stay low and near some of my brothers." Marie moved closer to the rest of the group to give them a few last instructions.

"Please, tell me that you know how to shoot a gun," Marcie said to Clarisse as she checked that her gun was fully loaded, and she then checked Clarisse's gun.

"Only a twenty-two years ago, but I think I can manage if I have to," Clarisse answered.

"I think you better plan on it," Marcie said, looking her firmly in the eye. "They may need our help, and by the way, our vacation is officially over. Try to stay behind me until you can pull yourself together."

CHAPTER TWENTY-FOUR

The siren on the building began wailing moments before the first shots rang out. A doctor and a lab assistant broke their cover and began to run across the lawn. Marie's brothers used their rifles and promptly dropped the two men in their tracks. Marie swiftly and accurately delivered a shot that silenced the outside amplifier of the security system.

"They don't ask many questions, do they?" Marcie whispered to Clarisse. "I think they are her brothers in arms. Father only confessed to having one child. No one has that many gun-toting brothers that don't even resemble one another."

Even in the midst of chaos, Marcie remained steady as a rock and was able to keep her glib confidence. Clarisse was trembling like a leaf and clinging as close as a shadow behind Marcie.

"Pull it together, Clarisse," Marcie whispered. "Things have gotten very real. It's important we at least live to fight another day."

More rapid shots rang out from within the building. It could only mean that the guards were still trying to halt the infiltration. Using the heavy rose trellis as a ladder, one of the brothers rapidly climbed to the second story and entered the building through an upstairs window.

A guard slipped out of the building and spotted movement in the bushes. His semi-automatic rained several rounds in their direction, but lightning flashed across the sky and disrupted his concentration. He dived for cover and avoided the return fire from several of Marie's brothers.

"This isn't looking good," Marcie whispered to Clarisse. "Keep down low. We are clearly outgunned in the hardware department."

Marie motioned to one of her brothers, Marcie and Clarisse. They silently edged closer to the main building under the cover of some nearby dense bushes.

A lab tech sprang out of nowhere and began firing, but Marie's shot hit him squarely before he could take any seriously, careful aim. A shot from inside the building was heard, and the guard with the semi-automatic rifle fell lifeless to the ground.

Marcie caught sight of a slight movement, in the overgrowth, on her left. She almost fired until she saw the man's cut-off sleeves. Marie's youngest brother ran up and joined them.

"Marie, I finished off the two clinic staff near the stables," her brother reported. "But I saw the dark-haired woman take off running toward the church."

Marie was immediately concerned about the priest, "Father Dubois is alone at the church."

Clarisse assured Marie, "I was there when Father locked and bolted both doors at the church. He has bars on the church windows."

Additional gunfire erupted from inside the building. The wind picked up once again, and rain began to spatter the ground. Marie was ready to make a final approach to enter the building when the four girls began emerging from the second-story window and climbing down the trellis. Two of the brothers followed their descent. Two additional shots were heard, and another brother limped out of the kitchen service door. He was wounded, but he had managed to kill the guard and take possession of his semi-automatic.

Several of Marie's brothers gathered whatever weapons their dead adversaries had left on the ground.

CHAPTER TWENTY-FIVE

The rain escalated as they gathered together. No one had seen the woman since she was spotted on foot moving toward the church. Two brothers took the maintenance truck and drove the four women and their wounded comrade over to the stable. They, and the files that Marie had salvaged, were immediately taken by others to a safe house in a nearby village. The maintenance truck, with the hope that it would provide them cover, was then used to cross the open grounds while approaching the church.

Marie warned them, "Time is short if the police are going to respond to the alarm." Marie was about to direct Marcie and Clarisse to head to where the horses were waiting when a small plane began to approach in the distance. "Wait here in the bushes," Marie said before she and several brothers ran to take cover closer to the building.

Marcie looked over at Clarisse. "You look like you're hanging together better. It's almost over. I hope Father is alright because he's got a lot of confessions to hear over all of this."

Clarisse looked at Marcie in disbelief.

"Don't mind me," Marcie responded. "At the moment, only threads of humor are holding me together."

The plane usually used the road as a runway. It came to a halt in front of the Ferme de Tayac and cut its engine. Two men deplaned, and within their visual area, nothing appeared amiss. They hurried through the rain, but when they came close to the main building, they caught the scent of gunpowder in the air. Marie, along with her brothers, swiftly circled around and dispatched both of the men. One of Marie's brothers approached the plane and boarded it.

Marcie and Clarisse were engrossed in watching the plane land; therefore, they failed to hear the women approach them from behind. Clarisse pulled the flask from her cargo pants, took a sip of water, and handed it to Marcie. Marcie swallowed several gulps and returned the flask. When they heard the sharp snap of a twig, they both turned. Although the woman's shot was aimed at Clarisse, it ricocheted off the flask, and the bullet hit Marcie squarely in the stomach, knocking her to the ground.

Clarisse didn't care that the woman was still aiming straight at her. She immediately reached and took Marcie's bandana and tried to stop the flow of blood. As Clarisse bent over Marcie with tears in her eyes, she heard Marcie whisper, "I refuse to be a fatted calf. Let me bleed out and bury me if I die and you survive." Marcie's face began to grey, but her eyes still reflected anger. "Don't let my heart go on beating in the chest of a New World Whoever." Marcie's breath became slow and then shallow. "The flask," she gasped weakly. Clarisse moved the water closer to Marcie, who tipped it so that some water poured over her wound. "Use the water on her," she murmured to Clarisse, struggling to say the words.

Clarisse rose from her knees. She turned to face the woman who had edged closer and still had her gun confidently pointed at Clarisse. Fury quickly rose inside Clarisse until it pulsed through every muscle in her body. Everything around her seemed to play out in slow motion when she aimed the flask at the woman. The water from the flask jettisoned forward at lightning speed until it hit the woman in the face and ran down her body. The water cut her like a red-hot surgical knife. As the woman fell to her knees, writhing with pain, Marcie picked up her gun, which still lay close to her, and placed a slug solidly in the woman's chest. Clarisse looked over at Marcie in disbelief.

Marcie was still lying on the ground, but now she was half propped up by her backpack. "I stopped bleeding," she said, with a shocked and quizzical look on her face. "It was the healing water." Confusion flashed across Marcie's face. "I just killed her, and we still don't even know her name."

Clarisse's hands were shaking when she bent down to look at Marcie's wound. It appeared to be sealed. Clarisse struggled to believe what her eyes beheld.

Father Dubois stepped out of the bushes, all but out of breath. The priest looked at the woman's body which was now utterly charred. "By Holy Water standards, she must have had a pretty shoddy soul. She would have died from the Holy Water alone. You only shortened her earthly suffering," he said to Marcie as he sat down on the ground beside her. "She could not gain access to the church. I followed her when she left the church, but as you know, I move at an incredibly slow pace, and she was running terribly fast."

Marcie locked eyes with the priest. "I believed the water would save me. Something told me to pour the water on my wound." She told him with astonishment. "I prayed and believed I would be saved."

"I thank God for that," Father said. "The water is selective at times. Depth of belief seems to be the key that unlocks its success." He took out his flask containing healing water and poured more of it on her wound. "After almost ninety years, I have finally been blessed to witness the miracle of the water."

Clarisse called out to Marie, "The woman is finished."

"Isn't that just how an accountant would sum things up," Marcie said with a sigh as Father Dubois helped her up into a sitting position.

"You have no idea how many prayers I said to keep all of you safe tonight," the priest said.

"You have no idea how busy your confessional is going to be," Marcie replied.

CHAPTER TWENTY-SIX

One sole opposing survivor was brought off of the plane. His hands were lifted high in the air, and a semi-automatic weapon was placed firmly at his back. Marie's brother called to her, "This one was hiding and insisted he only came to rescue his wife."

Marie stood in the open area as her brother brought the man from the plane while Father Dubois and Marcie approached behind her. Clarisse looked in the direction of the plane. Her first instinct was to run to him when she saw it was Roger. She hurried out from behind the bushes, but she slowed her pace when Marcie's words came back into focus. "They addressed someone who could be his double as Doctor at the clinic." She continued slowly walking towards Roger until they finally stood face to face.

The sharp, steady rain helped clarify Clarisse's thinking. The words of the priest became firmly fixed in Clarisse's head. "You must reach inside and gather your strength. Trust Marie."

"Thank God you are safe," Roger said. "I have been trying to call you." He reached for her as though he was going to take her in his arms, but she stepped back. He faltered at the look in her eyes. "I will always keep you safe, my love. I made sure no harm would come to you. You were to be treated like a princess."

"I have his business satchel," one of the brothers called and hurried it over to Marie.

Roger stood with his hands raised slightly and a gun still firmly planted in his back. Clarisse could see the edge of an identification tag under his jacket, so she reached to move the lapel of his suit coat to expose it. A garnet red fountain pen was in his dress shirt pocket. Thunder began to rumble as a determined look flashed across Roger's face. Clarisse sharply caught her breath and then steadied herself. "Dr. Rogerio Jourdain-Baulelaire," Clarisse read off of his identification.

A shot rang out, which enabled Marie to open Roger's briefcase.

Roger pleaded with Clarisse, "You don't know what a glorious world they have planned. Eventually, we would return home together, and then I can keep you safe." His voice wavered and began to hold traces of a hollow tone. "Don't you see? Whatever you want is yours. They will be good to us that way."

"This is the briefcase of your husband," Marie called to her. "He clearly is one of the Doctors of the World Order and part of the Jourdain family. The Jourdain family has plagued this part of France for hundreds of years. He is the specialty surgeon who rips the bodies of the Sang-real bloodline women apart to prolong the lives of the elite within their World Order."

Roger's expression reflected his desperation.

Remembering the envelope Roger was handed by the limo on their wedding night, Clarisse asked with tears of anger streaming down her face. "Did you sell me to them?"

Roger wiped at his eyes. "No, my love. They only bought a year of your time. It was a sacrifice they required of me to establish my elevation to the elite. You were to be one of the sacred ones. But now you are the virgin chosen to give birth to the new lord's child. Satordi received word today that you are the chosen bride." Roger continued with a confident edge of passion, "The scales that balance the world are about to weigh differently. It is our time now for the power of one. I pledged my very soul to become a member of the elite, and as my wife, you can have elite status too. It means you will survive and have a future. You should feel honored that you were chosen." There was a touch of sickening belligerence in his demeanor. It reached out and seemed to permeate the air around him. Roger's eyes suddenly turned stone cold when he realized that he had failed to gain any indication that she was agreeable. It was as if the Roger she knew no longer existed within his body.

Thunder rolled, and bile began to rise uneasily in Clarisse's stomach. "You knew this was all planned from the start?"

"Not the very start, but then somewhat," Roger answered. "You were not chosen to be the one until our wedding night."

"And the great plan includes that so many others should be dealt out like cuts of raw meat?" Clarisse asked Roger bitterly. Her knees had begun to weaken. She took the flask out of her cargo pants, took a sip of Holy Water to steady herself, and then her anger quickened. Clarisse then spit it in his face. He screamed as the droplets sizzled, burning deep caverns into his flesh. He fumbled with his pen until he released the pill and swallowed it just as Clarisse pulled the holy knife free from its wrapping within her pocket.

"He just took a cyanide pill. They all do when caught," Marie called out to Clarisse.

"It's time to meet your lord and mine," Clarisse said as she plunged the priest's dagger into his heart as the pill took effect. Lightning careened across the sky. She watched Roger fall and then stared in disbelief. A cloud of blackness burst forth from Roger, twisted in the air, and then dropped to the ground and dissipated into nothingness.

Flames suddenly leaped from Roger's wreathing body. Flashes of Clarisse's brief life with Roger cascaded through her mind. The moment they met, how secure she felt in his arms, his French songs, and the conservatory on their wedding day. She remembered how beautiful her wedding day was and how perfect they looked together in their photos. Memories of her short, deceit-based life with Roger overwhelmed her and then dissipated like the smoke that had filled the air around her.

The rain washed away any traces from her blood-stained hands. She began to feel cleansed as the raindrops hissed as they hit Roger's charred remains. Clarisse bent down, removed the knife, and numbly put it back in the leather wrapping. Nothing in the past months had been remotely close to the truth. As surely as hope had seemed to spring eternal, everything between them had now come to a final and fiery end.

Marie put an arm of comfort around Clarisse's slumped shoulders, "These are the saddest of times. There are bitter times ahead for all of us. The waging of a war against evil has begun. Unfortunately, we have many more to try and save. Many will fall, and some are chosen to fight when they least expect it. Faith in a better future world will make your spirit strong and brave beyond words. For now, you are safer with us. Welcome to the truth hidden in the South of France."

Clarisse inhaled deeply and searched for newfound strength from Marie's words and presence. She silently picked up Roger's fountain pen, which lay beside his ashes, and handed it to Marie. Thunder escalated but in the distance, and the rain diminished. Clarisse was soaked from the storm and began to shiver.

Father Dubois stepped forward with a dry, warm jacket for Clarisse and placed it around her shoulders. "The rain has stopped. The brothers brought this from the barn for you. One evil spirit at a time seems too difficult a task, but we have no choice but to inch into a better world. Come with me now, my child. Marie needs us to hurry to where the horses are gathered. I am riding with all of you."

After Clarisse mounted the dapple grey, Marcie handed her the reins and exhaled deeply. She exchanged glances with Clarisse. Marcie was wide-eyed, but she managed a weak smile. "I guess earning those leather-trimmed jeans was more imperative than either of us could have possibly imagined."

"Are you sure you are alright to ride?" Clarisse asked her.

"Amazingly, I'm fine," Marcie replied. "He took the pill Clarisse and killed himself. You only disposed of a demon inside of him. Are you alright to ride?"

"I desperately need to leave this place behind," sighed Clarisse as she made an effort to shake off her mental fog.

"Odd, but the only remaining sting concerns the lack of the other seven hundred and fifty dollars. I think we've both been had on that account," Marcie said.

"Spoken like a true American," Marie said, shaking her head. "Money is never far from your thoughts. Rest assured. We took whatever was in the safe at the Ferme. It does my heart good to reduce the coffers of their evil empire to any degree."

A sudden gust of wind burst upon them.

Marcie's horse grew restless. She reigned it in sharply. "I think that was the swift departure of our lives as we knew them. I can't even begin to guess where our roads might lead us."

"If we hurry," Marie interjected, "tonight, the road we travel leads eventually to shelter and our next warm meal."

The distant wail of a siren pierced the evening air.

Marie mounted her horse and reined it in until she faced the two of them. "Ride within the group with Father Dubois," she directed. "The three of you are best protected that way. We are half an hour to safety."

When they tapped their heels to their horse's flanks, their mounts surged forward, swiftly taking them beyond the nearest village and into the approaching darkness.

ABOUT THE AUTHOR

Although a native of Buffalo, New York, for most of her life, the author of this book also resided for ten years in a cabin deep in the bowels of Appalachian coal-mining country, close to nature, on the edge of Braddock's Run and the wilderness of the Savage Mountain. It was a well-learned lesson concerning how formidable wildlife, mother nature, and individuals can be.

The author never came face to face with a cougar in the mountains, but after her return to the Western New York area, she did have one wander into her naturalized backyard. True, but unbelievable to many, including the NYS Fish and Wildlife Department. The author gave in and began writing fiction when no one chose to believe her stories concerning actual events. So, it goes.

The author gardens profusely, wintering many plants in her home with an attached greenhouse room. The maximum she has cultivated a geranium is to a height of seven feet. Although there are photos, others treat this truth with skepticism. The author finds that the writing of fiction is similar to gardening. Some characters planted in a novel are allowed to flourish, some only fill in the necessary groundwork, and some are fated to die on the vine. Sometimes nurturing a character requires intense hoeing. Imagination should be cultivated daily.

The author's fictional writing interests range from the ancient past or current times to an imaginary future world. Following the lead of whatever inspires her, the author adheres to the principle that the reader always deserves a good ride. The author's unfinished stories reside in a folder entitled "Spits in the Wind."

Milton Keynes UK
Ingram Content Group UK Ltd.
UKHW020829270823
427433UK00001B/6

9 798891 217607